THE *Navajo* EVENT

Proof of God's Existence

RICK FISHMAN

outskirts
press

Outskirts Press, Inc.
http://www.outskirtspress.com

ISBN: 978-1-9772-5042-1

Library of Congress Control Number: 2022900155

Cover Photo © 2022 www.gettyimages.com. All rights reserved - used with permission.

Outskirts Press and the "OP" logo are trademarks belonging to Outskirts Press, Inc.

PRINTED IN THE UNITED STATES OF AMERICA

Publishers Cataloging-in-Publication
Fishman, Rick.

   The Navajo Event: Proof of God's Existence / by Rick Fishman – 1st ed.

        p. ; cm.

Audience: general
Summary: Worldwide debate ensues when a badly injured woman is healed by a Navajo medicine man and even the pope weighs in. Is it a miracle, or a monstrous hoax to get rich and cover up the murder of her husband?

        1. Paranormal—Fiction. 2. Suspense—Fiction. 3. Mystery—Fiction. 4. God—Fiction.

LCC PS 374.O28 2022
DDC 813/.54—dc23

Praise for *The Navajo Event*

"A page-turning story steeped in mysticism and intrigue: When a Navajo healing ceremony miraculously cures a burn victim, her family finds themselves entangled in a high stakes criminal investigation in Fishman's thrilling second novel. Fishman's characters are skillfully rendered, his prose is crisp, and the narrative is full of fast-paced, non-stop twists and turns. The plot is expertly structured to maximize tension and suspense—all of it feels authentic. At once funny and exhilarating, the book will appeal to lovers of fast-paced thrillers."

—*The Prairies Book Review*

"An entertaining mixture of fantasy and science fiction, the story demonstrates the author's creative imagination … and the fascinating pictures add to the tale. With no profanity or sex, readers might appreciate the (characters') over-the-top behaviors."

—*Online Book Club.Org*

"I really appreciate that the book brings together Jewish, Catholic, and Navajo traditions and let's them coexist peacefully … and does so without ever calling attention to itself for doing it. This book will find an audience that appreciates its off-the-wall antics and brief foray into the metaphysical."

—*SadieForsythe.Com Reviews*

Praise for *Sandlot Summit*

"Fishman's playful, well-written, and imaginative story ends with a life affirming message and the sweet hope of peace for all nations. This patriotic, engaging novel, will be a home run for readers of all ages."

—*Kirkus Discoveries*

"What a game! This is a funny novel full of spirit and laughter. It doesn't matter whether the reader is a baseball fan or not—the humor cannot be missed. The highly detailed full page illustrations are as humorous as the writing."

—*Allbooks Review*

To our daughter

Every moment with her is cherished.

Acknowledgements:

Special thanks to Dr. Robert Kaye who lived on the Navajo Reservation and provided a wealth of information on the subject.

Special thanks to Mr. Michael Kaye for his highly detailed editing and recommendations.

Special thanks to Mr. Wally Brown, a Navajo medicine man whose outstanding presentations on YouTube were my best source of information on Navajo culture.

Special thanks to my reviewers: Mr. Mark Russell, Ms. Judi Kaufman, Mrs. Marla Wolf, Mr. Steve Brofman

References:

Conchapman.wordpress.com – Patron saint of sandwiches

Tony Hillerman Portal – Navajo seal & Navajo customs

Tony Hillerman – The Blessingway, 2002 ebook – Navajo customs.

FronterasDesk.org – Diné College tries to save medicine people.

CatholicSentinel.org – The pope did not use bulletproof glass.

IdeaConnection.com, by Plan Box – Bucky paper used as heat shield.

YourDictionary.com – catharsis

Glosbe.com – English / Navajo dictionary

Navajo Nation Museum–Supreme beings are Diyin Dine'é, Holy people.

AdvocateHealth.com/assets/documents/faith/cg-native_american.pdf – A medicine man is considered a holy person.

https://www.qcc.cuny.edu/socialsciences/ppecorino/phil_of_religion_text/chapter_5_arguments - discussion of miracles and qualifications.

https://focusequip.org/how-does-someone-become-a-saint-a-5-step-process/ - Steps to becoming a saint.

https://www.lockheedmartin.com/en-us/news/features/2019-features/cleared-for-takeoff-hypersonic-flight.html - hypersonic info.

https://en.wikipedia.org/wiki/Hypersonic_flight -hypersonic info.

https://eos.org/research-spotlights/ - Single water molecules are a gas.

YouTube–The Vatican Archive – Holy Mass and Canonization of Mother Teresa of Calcutta- 9/4/2016

people.howstuffworks.com/question619-Sainthood recognizes what God has already done.

Photo Credits:

ONE

A stranger entered the sandwich shop wielding the largest hunting knife that the staff or customers had ever seen, and they froze in place as he stepped in the direction of the cash register.

The knife had a twelve-inch stainless steel serrated blade, so razor sharp that it would take only one slice to penetrate any object that got in its way... and one did.

His female companion, however, was not impressed.

"Logan, really, why can't you use a bagel guillotine like normal people?"

The man offered a flippant reply. "You know I'm not normal, love."

All present thought they were staring at Crocodile Dundee in a lab coat. This tall physician actually sported an attention-grabbing black safari hat complete with a band of crocodile teeth. He tipped it toward the dark blonde shift manager, Carli Green.

"Ma'am."

Carli thought she was too young to be called a ma'am and got right down to business, first, by reading their name tags. "Dr. Duncan, Dr. Dred, welcome to the Sandwich Condo. I have good news for you, Dr. Duncan. We're running a special today on silverware...so if you don't mind holstering your weapon, I can get started on your orders."

At five-foot-six, and rejecting any "diva" look, Carli had a pleasing appearance that blended in well almost anywhere. A recent graduate of The Ohio State University, majoring in psychology, she scoffed at any suggestion that she was wasting her degree...claiming that customer psychology and a killer smile kept the ovens warm and the cash register full, which helped her finish college almost debt free.

Her husband, Marty Newman, held a similar position as a server at a local steakhouse, and together, their incomes were sound enough to pay the bills. At the end of each workday, the two of them would spend a lot of time outdoors with their two energetic beagles, whom they named after the main characters in the *Peanuts* comic strip...Snoopy and Charlie Brown.

The couple had many friends at the townhouse apartment complex where they lived...and the grassy central courtyard was a great place to kick back and enjoy life.

TWO

Tommy the cat took his last sip of water for the night, made a final groom of his whiskers, and gingerly leaped to his spot on the left arm of the sofa…then the sofa exploded. Electrical fires are hard to predict. And if no one knew that months of plopping their bottoms down hard onto the cushions would cause one of the sofa toes to gradually shred the protective covering of a lamp cord…well, then they probably couldn't have predicted that a fifteen-pound cat would be the last additional weight needed to cause opposite bare wires to touch.

Everything that happened after that happened quickly. Caustic black smoke raced up the stairwell. The young married couple had been asleep upstairs in their townhouse apartment on the east side of Columbus, Ohio. When their smoke alarm sounded at 2:30 a.m., the top half of the bedroom was already filling with billowy poison. Neighbors in the adjacent apartment called 911 when they heard someone open the front window and yell "FIRE!"

The next to perish after the cat was the pair of dogs who shared their masters' bed and whose tiny lungs succumbed quickly to the smoke.

Much has been written (and a movie made) about the term "backdraft." When a fresh source of oxygen is offered to a fire, there will be an explosive burning of superheated gasses which loudly "whoosh" toward the source, in this case an open window. These gasses instantly seared the woman's back and the back of her arms while her husband desperately tried to beat out a flame that had lit the pants of his nightclothes. Their only means of escape was a twelve-foot drop out the front window.

Crowds of residents gathered. When fire engines and paramedics arrived minutes later, they reported finding a badly injured, but unidentified male and female, the first on the sidewalk, the second a few feet farther on the grass. And both were in a life-threatening condition. One of their friends, Libby, who also lived in the complex, was in tears and tried to tell first-responders that she knew their names. But with zero seconds to spare, the couple was placed on gurneys and then quickly, the two ambulances set off on the most direct route to The Ohio State University Medical Center.

THREE—POV Roland

Telephone bells at 7:30 a.m. rarely bring good news, and I could barely make out the quick, panicky remarks of Libby as she related the awful events of the past five hours.

No one can practice reacting to a family disaster, but in my job as an accountant for an auto parts company, I had trained myself to present an emotionless demeanor during the many occasions when I was chewed out by my boss (deserved or otherwise). I thanked Libby and told her we would be down there as soon as possible.

My wife, Laura, was already at her secretarial desk for her early start at an insurance firm in downtown Cleveland. Her usual cheerful voice answered my call, but when I gave her the news, she sobbed. I asked her to drive home carefully and we would get through this together. I hung up and began packing two small suitcases for the two-hour drive.

It was not much of a homecoming as we took the elevator to the sixth-floor Intensive Care Unit of the medical center. My daughter and I were both Ohio State graduates, but this was one part of the campus to which we had never ventured.

Apparently, they were expecting us. We were greeted immediately by a sturdy-looking five-foot-nine brunette who wore her hair in a top-bun. Add to that, thin eyebrows and bright red lipstick that bordered a practiced smile. She offered her hand.

"I'm Dr. Sabrina Dred, head of the ICU unit." She spoke in a smooth alto voice.

I took her hand. "Roland Green and my wife, Laura. I didn't recognize you as a doctor, with the lavender shirt."

"My apologies. It happens when two fast people with coffee run into each other. My lab coat is in the laundry. Let's go back to where we can talk privately," she suggested. Then she pressed a speed-dial number on her cell phone. "Dr. Duncan, can you please join us in the conference room?"

The plain room had four long tables arranged as a square to accommodate a large grouping if needed. There were also assorted medical presentation tools. We were seated at one of the corners.

"Before we begin, Mr. and Mrs. Green, I first want to reassure you that every member in our unit strives to provide the very best world-class care to all of our patients. When I arrive each morning, I say 'These patients are my children. What would I want for them?' They come to us broken. It's our job to fix them up—make them whole again—so they can go back to living normal, happy lives."

The doctor paused to open a bottled water and offered us two of the same.

"I can see that your daughter, Carli, is a real fighter…and youth is on her side; she's just twenty-one. But she's going to need a lot of support from both of you, especially emotionally. Most of our burn patients have PTSD, post-traumatic stress disorder. But we will provide Carli with the best psychological therapists, physical therapists…and every specialist required. She WILL get better."

Laura and I held hands. We nodded and said, "Thank you."

The surgeon's sudden entrance caught us by surprise.

He politely tipped his hat. "Mates," he greeted us with a smile.

Dr. Dred chimed in, "I'd like you folks to meet the finest spinal surgeon in Australia, Dr. Logan Duncan. He was looking for greater challenges, and fortunately for us, he chose to be a Buckeye. We're lucky to have him. In this building, he's like a rock star, and no one else is permitted to dress 'native' with a safari hat."

I stood, shaking his hand, and queried, "So your name 'Duncan' is like the yo-yo?"

"Right," he replied with an accent hitting the ear as 'royt.'

I don't know the difference between Cockney and Australian voices, but he did sound much like the little lizard on the Geico Insurance commercials.

He added, "But I'm here to talk about your daughter, Carli."

Dr. Duncan clipped one of Carli's x-rays to the light board on the wall and turned it on. From inside his lab coat he took out his 'pointer,' a very sharp twelve-inch, shining, steel-bladed hunting knife.

I mumbled to myself, "This guy really stays in character." Then I asked him, "Dr. Duncan, do you use that knife in surgery?"

"What, this? Naw," he scoffed. "I only use it for hunting crocs…and for blokes who try to cross me."

The surgeon then placed his blade tip on part of the x-ray. "This is where she has a compression fracture of the L2 segment."

His remark startled me. "Wait! You're saying Carli broke her back?! We didn't know anything about that!"

"Relax, mate," he replied. "It's not too bad. She can already wiggle

4

her toes, so no nerve damage. But you see how the L2 vertebra looks a bit squashed compared to the others? Well, you just can't leave it like that. She could end up with spondylolisthesis."

"Huh?"

"Slippage of the spine. But no worries, mate. Spinal fusion surgery is my bread and butter. Take a look at today's technology."

Dr. Duncan took a plastic box out of his pocket and showed me its contents…four four-centimeter screws, metallic silver in color, and two longer rods.

"Titanium screws," he continued, "are strong, light weight, and non-toxic…and they'll last a very long time. Now if you were the doctor, which four spine segments would you drill them into?"

"I have no clue."

"Well, since you have four screws, why don't we try the two above and the two below the bad one?"

I looked at the x-ray labels and recited, "The two above are T12 and L1, and the two below are L3 and L4."

"You'll make a fine surgeon, mate," he chuckled. "Now once we connect all four screws to the rods, she'll be able to hop, skip, and jump to her heart's content…after a period of rehab of course. So once the good Dr. Sabrina here and her crew get Carli's vitals stabilized, they'll be rolling her right down to my O.R. (operating room)…probably in a couple of days. Nice meeting you folks."

Dr. Duncan put the weapon back inside his lab coat, tipped his hat again, and saw himself to the door.

Dr. Dred folded her hands and continued our consultation. "Dr. Duncan can act a little too happy sometimes. I'll be honest with you, Mr. and Mrs. Green…the chances of a burn patient surviving the first twenty-four hours is an 'inverse' of the affected area. In other words, since Carli has second and third degree burns over 30% of her body, then she has a 70% chance of survival. But I really believe she'll be 100%. So now it's time for us to go see Carli, but I want to prepare you first so that you understand this will not be the Carli you're used to seeing. She's in bad shape. The care here is intensive for a reason."

I nodded.

"Visiting hours are unlimited. You can use the recliners in the waiting room if you'd like to nap. Hot chocolate and coffee there is always free, and

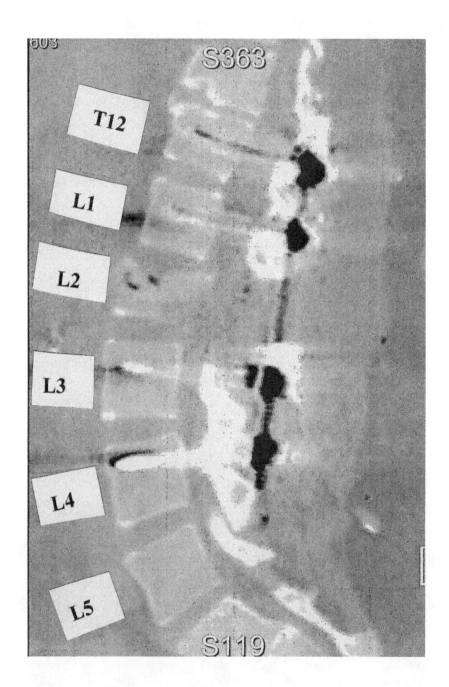

a fruit bowl comes at 3:00 p.m. Don't hesitate to ask questions. We're here to help families as well as patients."

As we exited the conference room, I whispered to my wife, "Dr. Dred is very nice."

Laura agreed. "She's wonderful."

Dr. Dred led us past the ICU reception desk and down the first hallway of rooms ... But we immediately stopped in our tracks. Hayward and Hally Newman looked at us and shook their heads as a white sheet was placed over their son's body in Room 1.

"Marty didn't make it," his father sobbed.

The two of us embraced, and with difficulty I got out the few words, "I am so sorry."

Laura did the same with Mrs. Newman.

"Good luck with Carli," Hayward told me. "We all love her."

Dr. Dred's mouth hung open. "Oooh folks, forgive me. When they came in, I saw they had different last names, so I had no idea—"

I interrupted, "They'd been married for two years."

The doctor echoed, "I'm so sorry…I'm so sorry."

Hayward urged me away. "Go…take care of Carli."

I was already feeling survivor's guilt. We moved down the hall till we found a door sign indicating that our daughter occupied ICU Room 8. Dr. Dred instructed us to "gown up" before entering as she explained, "Staph infections are all too common."

Laura and I tied off each other's isolation gown in the back. Then we donned the required surgical masks and latex gloves. I took a deep breath as Dr. Dred pulled back the curtain.

Then I felt my stomach drop as if plummeting down a roller coaster. Was this really our Carli? Every limb was wrapped in heavy white gauze. Her face, with eyes closed, was nearly beet red. Her blonde hair had been singed to a brownish purple with black crinkled edges. The black smudges around her orbital sockets gave her the look of an apparition. I was not trying to humor myself when I thought that she looked like a cast member of the *Addams Family*.

Dr. Dred explained, "Don't be alarmed by her outward appearance. Her face is not burned, and everything on it will clear up in a few days. The apparatus in her mouth is an endotracheal tube. It's helping her breathe and, as you can see, it's also sucking out the black liquid smoke residue from her lungs."

The doctor then approached the bed and spoke softly. "Carli…Mom and Dad are here."

After a few moments, her eyes opened with a glassy stare. She didn't try to look for us. Laura and I moved forward.

"Hello, dear…hello, kiddo," we said sweetly.

"She's been heavily sedated," the doctor pointed out, "and might not be able to communicate for a while."

Suddenly, Carli's eyes opened wide and she looked at us with panic. Her bandaged arms started flapping up and down. "Maahh EEE Ehhh."

The sounds were animal-like, emerging from her throat in a low, raspy grunt. Dr. Dred adjusted the mouth tube to help her out.

Carli tried again, only louder. "MAAHH…EEE…DEHHH!"

I bent down and whispered to her, "Are you trying to ask us if Marty's dead?"

It took a moment for her to catch her breath, but she nodded her head.

Laura grabbed my shoulder. "Roland, we weren't going to talk about that yet."

I shook my head. "She wants the truth, Laura, and we owe her that…I'm so sorry, baby, but Marty didn't make it."

My daughter closed her eyes and went to sleep.

FOUR

For the next two days, life in the ICU evolved into a routine. After Carli survived the first twenty-four hours, her condition was upgraded from 'critical' to 'serious.' We were told that's an improvement. Twice a day, she would be transported by a shower trolley to a bathing room on the fourth floor. With the last of the smoke residue sucked out, the trachea tube was removed from her throat.

As nurses explained, the trolley was a modified gurney topped with an open rubber container large enough for a person to lie in warm water. The bandages would then be changed as the burn wounds were gently cleaned. This was necessary to prevent bacterial infection.

I thought about the emotional toll that all of these hospital workers endured as part of their daily jobs. I was just thankful they were there for us.

But Laura and I hated it when Carli was transported out of the room. She would always look back at us with empty eyes and say, "Daddy, I'm scared." Yes, Daddy was the go-to parent for all the scary stuff…like thunder rumbles, or any giant, hideous bug flying around in her bedroom. We both held her hand and reassured her we would always be there for her…and that we would get through it together.

During this "break" time for us, we took the elevator down to get some fresh air. How ironic, we thought, that Carli's employer, the Sandwich Condo, was directly across the street from the hospital. Sometime during the last three years, she must have met nearly all the medical personnel who were caring for her now.

When we walked in, all the employees surrounded us, some in tears. They gave us hugs, asking us to transfer those hugs back to their co-worker. Carli's boss insisted that we eat here free of charge for the duration of her hospital stay. Then he gave us an envelope with money, saying, "We all want to feel that we're doing something to help."

Laura and I were touched, and there weren't enough thank-yous in our vocabulary to express our appreciation.

* * *

On the fourth day, Laura and I left the hospital at 10:00 a.m. to attend the funeral of Marty Newman in Pickerington, Ohio, a suburb of Columbus. As we joined along in the motorcade, I was surprised to see that the townsfolk of central Ohio would pause along the route and salute our procession. It's something we never witnessed in northern Ohio.

9

When we arrived at the cemetery, we did not expect to see so many of our friends and family from the Cleveland area. They all said they wanted to be here to support both families, and we thanked them for that.

I recalled that when an elderly person died, the aftermath of the service could be filled with all sorts of smiles and laughter, celebrating the achievements of a long and cherished life. But when a young person dies, there are few smiles.

After a light lunch at the Newmans' home, we graciously excused ourselves to return to Carli's apartment to retrieve any salvageable personal effects, all of which were covered in heavy black soot...a visit we hoped never to repeat.

When we returned to her bedside, the crocodile-hunting surgeon was already standing over her, checking off items on his clip-board.

"Good news, folks," he said cheerily, "It's showtime. Dr. Dred says that Carli is now strong enough for surgery and she's green-lighted her for 6:00 tomorrow morning. We're prepping the OR as I speak, and Carli is patient number one on the docket."

"Oh, that's *great* news," Laura responded.

"Thank you, Doctor," I added.

Carli was still too sedated to understand what was going on, but we held her hands...with the hope that she was about to turn the corner.

* * *

The fifth day was a very good day. Laura and I visited the sandwich shop for lunch and let all of Carli's co-workers know of her progress.

We waited patiently for the nine-hour surgery to be completed. Dr. Duncan entered the ICU waiting room at 3:00 p.m. and handed us a paper copy of Carli's x-ray.

"There you go, folks," he said confidently. "Pretty as a picture. You can see here how the four screws are drilled right through the centers of T12, L1, L3, and L4...just like you instructed me, Mr. Green."

I grinned. "Yeah, right."

"The rods hold them all together as one unit, and that leaves the compressed segment, L2, floating all by its lonesome with no more pressure. That should relieve a lot of Carli's pain."

I shook his hand. "We can't thank you enough, Doctor."

"No problem, mate...As soon as she's out of post-op, they'll wheel her back to Room 8. You folks take care now."

Dr. Duncan tipped his safari hat once more and departed.

FIVE

The sixth day started out routinely enough. Carli was still somewhat groggy as the medical staff tried to wean her off the morphine and other powerful pain medications. She was still heavily bandaged for the burns and didn't feel like saying much, but the spinal surgery seemed to have gone well.

At 10:00 a.m., one of the nurses dropped into Room 8 and said, "Mr. Green, you have some visitors in the waiting room who would like to see you."

I turned to Laura. She nodded and said, "Go ahead, I'll stay with Carli."

To say that I was surprised to see my five visitors would be an understatement. Dr. Bill Green, my first cousin, worked as a physician on the Navajo Reservation in northeast Arizona. Accompanying him were four members of the tribe, three of whom I recognized, although it had been five years since our family had paid them all a visit during an "out West" vacation trek.

SHASH SHiMá, known to all as Mama Bear, was our favorite…a somewhat plump folk singer who wore a denim jacket over a voluminous body dress. Numerous forms of Native jewelry adorned her wrists, neck, and earlobes. She approached and gave me a squeeze I'd remember…and when she laughed, she laughed loudly.

"We've missed you guys, Roland," she said with a broad smile. "With Dr. Bill living nearby us, you're like extended family." She turned and pointed to a young lady. "You remember DóLii YáZHí, Little Bluebird? My daughter was just a skinny little thing when you last saw her. Now I'm trying to find her a hubby."

"Oh, stop it, Mama." The girl blushed. "Just keep teaching me to sing."

The large woman turned back. "Roland, do you remember my son AGAAN 'AA HASTí, Caring Arms? Maybe not. He was only twelve when you saw him last, and back then, we were still calling him SHASH YáZHí, Little Bear. He uses his 'caring arms' on that drum he carries…and you won't see him without it."

Along with the drum, the handsome young man sported a purple shirt, denim jeans, short hair, and a white headband. He smiled and nodded his head for a greeting.

The fourth member of the small group needed no introduction. HA'íí'ááGO, Rising Sun, was the most revered medicine man of the Navajo Nation. Though short in stature, this regal and dignified tribal elder was the loving grandfather to an entire people.

11

No justice could be done in extolling his presence. The kindly face with leathery skin made no attempt to disguise his ninety-four years. The medicine man wore a solid red flannel shirt, black pants, leather moccasins, and a wide black headband. What stood out most, though, was the copious number of turquoise jewels that managed to fill all the appropriate showplaces that a human being would care to decorate. Along with a silver and blue beaded belt that displayed several rising suns, there was an assortment of shining geometric figures and animal shapes that assigned themselves to fingers, wrists, ears, and biceps.

But the pendant he wore around his neck was unmistakably coruscating, meant to reflect brilliance in any lighting, with each jewel counting a unique number of facets. At the center, hanging near his navel, was a smooth black rectangular stone, about five inches long, with each of the eight corners held in place by a claw setting or prong.

I remembered that proper etiquette was to *not* look him in the eye, so I halfway bowed my head and said, "Rising Sun, I am honored to see you again."

He did not smile, but instead, offered a straight hand. I extended mine, only enough to properly allow our fingers to touch, and then slip back toward their owners.

Bill put his arm around my shoulder and said quietly, "We need to talk over in the corner."

"Did you fly out here on your own?" I asked him.

"Is there any other way to travel?" he shot back. "I bought a Piper Saratoga last year…six-seater…a nice upgrade from my last plane."

"You guys are about the last people I expected a visit from."

In the corner of the waiting room, Bill whispered, "Roland, this is serious business, and we don't have a lot of time. I've got many patients waiting for me back in Chinle, the town where we live. Rising Sun is here to perform a Navajo healing ceremony on Carli. It's called a Blessingway rite."

"What?" I said, almost in disbelief. "I don't understand."

"Roland, I'm sure your rabbi would approve. Here, take a look at this photo."

"Ugh!" I immediately turned away when I saw the grotesque image.

Bill continued, "Four years ago, the boy in the photo was in a farming accident on the reservation. He was trying to unclog the blades on a threshing machine when the engine accidentally started up again. Both his forearms were cut off, and his hands were badly mangled. He was able to walk back to my clinic, and I tied off the stumps while others went to retrieve the severed forearms."

I shook my head with pity and asked, "Why are you showing me this?"

Bill turned me about-face and pointed to the young man who was lightly tapping on his drum. "Roland, it was my seventh time witnessing his Navajo healing ceremony, but this one blew me away."

My eyes widened as I looked closer at the boy who had beautiful fingers and not so much as a scar on either arm. I whispered, "But that's impossible!"

Bill nodded. "You're right. It's impossible...except I witnessed it with my own eyes. The ceremony took a lot out of Rising Sun, and he needed three days to recover. Roland, I'm really not sure if he's capable of helping Carli. He's ninety-four, but he asked me to bring him here to give it a try...to do a good deed."

"Bill, that scares me. I don't want the man dying of a heart attack while he's trying to help my daughter."

"That's not your decision, Roland...nor mine...but his alone. And it would be extraordinarily rude of us to turn him away upon being offered such a powerful and personal healing gift. Carli would be the first BiLAGáANA, meaning Caucasian, to receive the ceremony."

"Why is that?"

"Because the Navajo generally aren't too fond of the white Europeans who decimated Indian populations across America. Carli is *my* family, so they regard her as *their* family too."

I paused to consider a decision. "Would they need to poke and prod her?"

"It's a musical ceremony. No one would touch her, and the whole thing will be over in ten minutes...but no witnesses."

I shook my head vehemently. "No, Bill! I don't know these people that well. I *have* to be there for my daughter."

Bill walked over to Rising Sun and whispered in his ear. Rising Sun whispered back.

"Okay, Roland," said Bill. "You can stay in the back corner of her room. But you must promise not to move a muscle and not to say a word during the entire ceremony. Doing so could jeopardize Carli's life."

My eyes widened. "Okay, now I'm *really* scared."

Rising Sun

"Don't be, Roland. This is a good thing. I promise you."

I took a deep breath. "This is going to hit Laura like a thunderbolt. But first, let me go back there and see if I can clear it with the head of ICU."

Bill nodded, and in a few minutes I returned with a broadly beaming Dr. Sabrina Dred.

"Hello and welcome!" she gushed. "We are absolutely ecstatic that the Navajo Nation has sent representatives to honor our facility with their presence."

I briefly introduced each member of the Navajo entourage and added, "Dr. Dred, my cousin here, Dr. Bill Green, flew them here in his own small plane for the occasion."

She answered, "Mr. Green and Dr. Green, you have an amazing and loving family, and this is exactly the kind of activity we encourage to raise the spirits of our patients. We are thrilled that you are all here. By any chance, would I be allowed to watch the healing ceremony?"

"I'm sorry, Dr. Dred," said Bill. "Tribal custom says no one except for immediate family."

"That's perfectly fine," she replied. "Not a problem. Let me just check Carli's schedule…Okay, she's got shower trolley in thirty minutes. Will that be enough time for you?"

"Yes," answered my cousin, "the ceremony today will only take ten minutes."

"Perfect, then let's head back there now. You might draw a little attention, but I'll clear a path for you. Are your guests comfortable with following protocol and gowning up with masks and gloves?"

Rising Sun answered with a nod.

As we headed down the ICU hall, I turned and noted to my cousin, "Bill, I have to say that Dr. Dred is the nicest doctor we have ever met. ICU can be a sad place, but she always knows how to lift our mood…and make the surroundings seem, you know, brighter. She just exudes joy every time she speaks."

"That's a nice luxury, Roland," he replied. "You're lucky to have her… Oh, before I forget, here's a sheet with the English lyrics of the healing song they'll be singing in Navajo. You can follow along. Most ceremonies take several hours or even days to complete, but we have to be practical time-wise, with so many patients waiting back home. So Rising Sun will get right down to business."

The walk a few doors down had me quickly saying, "Hi honey, we have some old friends visiting here whom we met five years ago on vacation. You remember my cousin, Bill. Why don't you join us outside the room while we all gown up?"

Laura's eyes darted back and forth in confusion. "Roland, what's going on here?"

I didn't even bother introducing the tribe. "Laura, good news…The medicine man here, Rising Sun, will perform a Navajo healing ceremony for Carli, and that's really a wonderful thing…So if you can just wait outside here with Bill, it'll be all done in a few minutes."

"Roland!" she exclaimed. "What's wrong with you? You don't think you need to consult me on something as weird as this? Carli's finally sleeping. You can't just go in there and wake her up."

With my safety garb on, I took hold of her wrists and stated, "I'm sorry for the short notice, honey. I didn't know this was coming myself, but it is really, really important that we perform this healing ceremony. These folks from the Navajo Nation came all the way from Arizona to do this good deed for us. We absolutely need to trust Bill on this one."

My wife was still extremely peeved and she snapped at me, "Then explain why I'm being kicked out, but you get to go in."

"It's a cultural bylaw," Bill interrupted. "If the medicine man were to drop dead, then a male over eighteen must be on hand to complete the ceremony."

I knew that was total bull, but my cousin wasted no time in ushering the five of us into ICU room 8 and shutting the door all the way. As promised, I took my spot in the far corner while the Navajo quartet gave Carli about four feet of room as they moved to their positions, the medicine man toward the south and women toward the southwest. Prayer sticks were placed toward the east. Caring Arms stood north with his drum.

The ceremony began immediately. Rising Sun placed his hands over his heart while Caring Arms began a soulful repetition on his tom-tom. Often, the medicine man will sing. In fact, the Navajo word for medicine man is HATAALLii, meaning "singer." But with the facemask, I couldn't tell if Rising Sun was singing or not. Today, Mama Bear and Bluebird were quite audible, especially with Bluebird shaking the sacred gourd rattle. I read my lyrics sheet as they sang the healing song called the "Night Chant" in their native tongue.

House made of light.
House made of mist.
House made of zigzag lightning stands high upon it.
Your offering I make.
Restore my feet for me.
Restore my legs for me.
Restore my body for me.
Restore my mind for me.
This very day, take out your spell for me.
You have taken it away from me.
Far off it has gone, happily I recover.
No longer sore may I walk.
Happily may I walk.
Impervious to pain, may I walk.
With lively feeling may I walk.
As it used to be long ago, may I walk.
May it be beautiful before me.
May it be beautiful behind me.
May it be beautiful below me.
May it be beautiful above me.
May it be beautiful all around me.
In beauty, it is finished.

As their melodic voices continued, I became mesmerized by the "special effects" taking place above Carli's body. Three powerful stimuli appeared to be emulating the first three lines of verse…one at a time.

First came the light…a bright wall of light that assumed the shape of a human (Carli) and extended downward from near the ceiling to Carli's body on the bed. I guess it didn't matter that Carli was under a cover.

Then came the mist, or tiny water droplets. I couldn't understand how they were just hanging in the air in the same space that the light had occupied. I had to give Rising Sun credit for creating some pretty nice accompaniments to the music.

Finally, the zigzag lightning looked similar to Fourth of July sparklers… only lots of them. They, too, took up the same three-dimensional space above Carli's body that the light and mist had done before them.

This was a stunningly beautiful ceremony and it was over way too quickly. Carli wasn't even awake for it.

I expressed my thanks to Rising Sun and his three companions. But when I opened the door to exit, my wife was standing there piercing me with a scowl…and with her arms folded across her chest.

"Roland, it's bad enough when you do crazy things on your own, but when it concerns our daughter, I expect to be consulted first."

"Honey—"

"Don't 'honey' me."

"Laura, I'm sorry. These Navajo people had met Carli and they loved her, and they wanted to do something to try to help. I'm sorry they were under such a time crunch or it would have been a better visit."

While we argued, Bill was quickly ripping off the gowns and gloves from his small group. I started walking and thanking him at the same time. "Bill, I really do appreciate the generosity of these Navajo people. This was a great gesture on their part."

Bill smiled and handed me his business card. "Keep me posted on Carli's condition. We'll all be rooting for her…Sorry for the rush, but we've got to get back home."

My cousin and the young man flanked an obviously exhausted medicine man and helped him move down the ICU hallway. I marched with them and waved as they departed the waiting room.

SIX

Twenty minutes after the ceremony, the shower trolley arrived on schedule and Carli groggily got out the words, "See ya later."

We both kissed her on her forehead and answered back, "See ya soon."

It was break time again and we headed back to the waiting room for some coffee and a snack. Little did we know, our routine was about to change dramatically.

Brad Banner, one of the male nurses in the bathing room assigned to changing bandages, had a look of puzzlement on his face. He paused in the middle of his work. Then he nudged the woman a bit but she did not respond. She was, however, still breathing fine. There was no emergency, but something wasn't right. He punched up a number on his cell phone.

"Hello, Dr. Dred?...Hi, this is Brad Banner stationed in the bathing room. Um, I think you guys made a mistake and sent us over the wrong patient."

"Wrong patient?" the doctor responded with surprise. "What are you talking about, a joke? No one makes a fool out of *me*, Brad."

"No ma'am. According to my chart, you were supposed to send over a burn patient named Carli Green. But the woman we checked in has no burn wounds...anywhere."

"Are you sure? You don't want to see me go ballistic, do you? This will be a career-ender if you're wrong."

"Positive."

"Don't move. I'll be right over."

Dr. Dred hung up and sprinted down the ICU hallway to verify Carli's absence from Room 8. She checked all the other rooms too just to be sure. Then she bolted out of ICU into the main corridor and ran to the stairwell, as the elevators were far too slow for her current mission. She leaped the stair sections, bumping into walls just to rebound her body to the next set of steps. Then, flying down the fourth-floor corridor, she yelled out, "GANGWAY!" at a highly startled selection of doctors, patients, and visitors. They froze against the walls as the maniacal sprinter brushed past them in her white lab coat.

Dr. Dred burst into the bathing room as Brad Banner pointed the way. With disbelief, she leaned closer and examined the woman's back. "Who are you?" she asked. With no response, Dr. Dred grabbed the woman's shoulders and shook her violently.

"WHO ARE YOU?" she again demanded.

The woman coughed twice and then answered quietly, "Carli Green."

"No you're not!" the doctor snapped back. "Your hospital wrist band might say 'Carli Green,' but your back is smooth. You don't even have a scar from yesterday's spinal surgery."

Punching up her cell phone, the doctor called out loudly, "Security! This is Dr. Dred, ICU...I'm initiating a code yellow, missing patient, sixth floor...probable kidnapping...name, Carli Green...burn patient...white female, five-six, blonde, blue."

"Copy that."

"And I want this entire hospital put on lockdown immediately...all exits. No one goes in or out without my authority...and I need two guards sent to the bathing room now...and I want three guards sent to the ICU conference room to wait for me."

"Acknowledged."

"Wow," said Brad Banner. "What do think is going on, Doc?"

"I don't know, Brad. But I guarantee you that I'm going to find out."

Her next call went to her assistant. "Janet, would you call the Columbus office of the FBI and tell them we need assistance? Just say there's been a kidnapping...yes, really...and ask Dr. Stanton to come down too when he has a chance...Yes, I know that the chairman of a hospital is always busy, but tell him it's important...Okay, and then call the Port Columbus airport security office and tell them to be on the lookout for four Navajo Indians and a Caucasian pilot who are trying to escape in a small plane. They must be stopped from taking off. Thanks."

When the two guards arrived shortly, Dr. Dred instructed them, "Take this woman to the eighth floor and get her a room."

"Seriously, Doc?" exclaimed the male nurse. "You're sending her to the 'naughty ward'?"

"Brad, this is a full service hospital. Sometimes, even criminals deserve quality medical care."

* * *

Back in the ICU waiting room, Laura and I wondered about the buzzer and the intercom calling out, "AAAAAH...AAAAAH...CODE YELLOW... SIXTH FLOOR."

Dr. Dred approached us. "Both of you follow me," she ordered gruffly.

We looked at each other, thinking, "What happened to the 'fun' doctor?"

20

It was back to the conference room, only this time, my heart started thumping when I saw three police officers sitting off to the side. The atmosphere reminded me of being sent to the principal's office at school.

"Is something wrong?" I asked meekly.

"Sit down," Dr. Dred directed.

My wife and I took seats a couple of feet apart from each other. Dr. Dred walked behind us and stood by my left. Then she moved, standing near my right, and leaning over...I felt her breathing down my neck. It was starting to creep me out.

Suddenly, she slammed her right hand onto the table and screamed, "WHERE IS SHE?!"

Both of us nearly jumped out of our seats. I turned around and saw the wild look in the doctor's eyes. I didn't know what she meant. I didn't know what to say.

"Just tell me where she is, Mr. Green," she repeated.

"Where's who?" I asked quietly.

The doctor spat back, "'Where's who' is the wrong answer!"

Dr. Dred

Then she stood behind me again, stalking me like her prey. I certainly wasn't expecting her to dig her fingernails into the trapezius muscles in my back. Ow, that hurt. Wasn't this considered an assault? The police officers didn't seem to be making any attempt to intervene. *They* sure knew who was boss. And now, I knew.

"Listen carefully, Mr. Green," she spoke directly into my right ear. "You may think you're a really smart guy flim-flamming your way past the rubes up in Cleveland…but here in central Ohio, and especially in this medical facility, nothing gets past *me*."

Dr. Dred released her unpleasant grip and walked to the back of the room to borrow a pair of handcuffs from one of the officers. She threw them on the table in front of me. "Here, put these on," she ordered.

"No way!" I shot back. "You're no policeman."

"But I know a policeman," she replied, pointing back to the officer. "If you don't want to wear bracelets, then you might want to start thinking about co-operating."

"Okay, okay," I answered, as my anxiety level was really building. "You want to know where she is…Okay, so you're looking for a woman…and the name of the woman is…?"

"Carli Green."

"Our daughter?" Laura clamored with alarm. "What did you do with our daughter?"

"Zip it, missy," Dr. Dred hissed at my wife. "You're not a suspect in this."

"Suspect in WHAT?" I yelled. "We thought she was with your staff. The last time we saw her, she was on the shower trolley. We kissed her forehead and said 'See ya soon.'"

"As you well know, Mr. Green, that was an imposter…whom we've locked up in the prison ward on the eighth floor."

Laura stood up quickly and bellowed, "I want to see my daughter NOW!"

Dr. Dred was just fine with that request. She pointed to an officer and said, "Please escort Mrs. Green to the naughty ward and allow her to visit with her alleged daughter."

"Why do you think she's an imposter?" I asked the doctor.

"Is that a rhetorical question, Mr. Green, one for which you already know the answer? You were the only witness. You were there when the bodies were swapped."

"That's crazy!"

"Is it? You had to be in on it. You and those Navajos make a nice little conspiracy of five. And by continuing your denials, you're only making it harder for yourself. So why don't you just be a good boy and tell Dr. Dred how you switched the bodies."

"I'll repeat…this is crazy."

"In fact, I don't even think those were real Indians. You just hired them to help pull off your hoax."

"I'm offended by your words, Doctor. Those people are gentle, loving, and real members of the Navajo Nation. They came here to help Carli."

"Oh, and indeed they did. Why don't we take a look at the security footage when they left Room 8?"

Dr. Dred retrieved one of the laptop computers from off a shelf. With a bit of pointing and clicking, she came upon the section where the Navajos were departing down the ICU hallway after the ceremony.

"Hmmm…" she mumbled, holding her chin in her hand. Then she suddenly cried out, "OH! I think I've got you, Mr. Green."

The doctor flipped the laptop around so I could see the screen. "Do you see the size of Mama Bear's dress?" she asked. "You could easily hide a human being under that…and that's how you switched the bodies." She slapped the laptop shut. "Case solved!" she called out to the two police officers. "Mr. Green, you can put the handcuffs on now, and we'll just wait for the FBI to pick you up."

Now my face turned red with rage. "Dr. Dred! Have you ever heard of a thing called 'due process'?"

The doctor sat down next to me and crossed her arms. She looked at me with a smug satisfaction. "Twin, triplet, or clone? Take your pick, Mr. Green. You should know which is correct…unless you kidnapped her as an infant. A blondie born to two brown-haired parents? Just how many skeletons *are* there in your closet, Mr. Green?"

"Stop it. And Carli doesn't have a twin anyway," I informed her. "She was a C-section baby and I was right there in the operating room when she was born. When the doctor wrapped her up in a little blanket and handed her to me, he said 'You have a lady baby.' I swear, no other babies came out of Laura's womb."

"Well, that's easy enough to check out."

Once again, Dr. Dred punched up her assistant's number. "Hi, Janet. I want you to check out the birth registry of Carli Green, age twenty-one, born at—"

23

When the doctor's eyes looked up at me, I filled in, "Hillcrest Hospital, Mayfield Heights, Ohio."

"Did you get that, Janet? Good, call me back when you have an answer."

"Either way," she added, "what made you think you could get away with such a ridiculous hoax as this? Remember 'Balloon Boy'? The father dialed 911 and was frantically telling authorities that his six-year-old son had climbed aboard a homemade helium balloon shaped like a flying saucer and it accidentally took off. It immediately attracted worldwide attention...public fascination. Oh, this poor boy! How will he survive such a terrible ordeal? Well, it turned out that the little darling was hiding in the attic the whole time and when he came out, he asked, 'Are we still doing this for the show?'"

"Yes, I remember that."

"And did you remember that the father was charged with a felony and had to go to jail...and pay a very large fine?"

"Yes, I remember."

"Well, then how does that square with you, Mr. Green? If you had one tenth the brains of an amoeba, you'd have realized that your plan was *also* doomed from the start. You're running around yelling 'Oh, my poor daughter! She lost her husband and her little doggies and a cat.' You were hoping to pull on the public's heartstrings, weren't you?"

"Stop it. I've done nothing of the sort."

"Oh, but that was the plan all along, was it not? You'll get your worldwide attention, Mr. Green...but not the type you were seeking. The only thing missing is a catchy nametag like 'Balloon Boy.' Hmmm...How about 'Mr. Green's Navajo Event?' Is that catchy enough? Why don't you tell me exactly what you saw during your 'Event'?"

I took a deep breath. "Well, the two ladies were doing the singing of the healing song with a gourd rattle. The boy was keeping the beat with his drum. And Rising Sun, the medicine man, had his eyes closed with his hands over his heart and was concentrating very hard."

"Is that all?"

"Well, there was 'stuff' happening over Carli's body."

"Stuff? What kind of stuff?"

"Well, it looked like it came down from the ceiling. There was bright light for a couple of minutes, and then some water droplets, and then something that looked like sparklers."

"So let me get this straight. Your daughter was being attacked by flash-lights, squirt guns, and Fourth of July sparklers, and you just sat there and did nothing?"

"I thought they were magic tricks that were part of the ceremony. I was told not to do or say anything."

"And you always do as you're told, don't you?"

The doctor's cell phone rang. "Yes, Janet? Uh huh…okay, then go ahead and cancel the code yellow and the lockdown…Thanks."

Dr. Dred began hovering over my back again…from left to right. Then her 'talons' grabbed my shoulders as they did earlier. "Why, you tricky little devil," she scolded. "Maybe I underestimated you. You're much more clever than I imagined. It turns out that Carli does *not* have a twin."

I was exhaustively annoyed now and mumbled, "Well, duhhhh."

Dr. Dred released me and walked over to the light board, where she re-attached Carli's two x-rays.

"So this is before and after the spinal surgery," the doctor pointed out. She put her hand on her chin and studied the two images.

"Absolutely amazing," she uttered. Then she pointed at the second image and declared, "This surgery had to be faked. It's obvious that Dr. Duncan never performed an operation on your daughter. What we're looking at here on the x-ray has to be a cadaver…or cadaver spine. Am I correct, Mr. Green? Is Dr. Duncan somehow in cahoots with your little conspiracy? Although… what should we expect from a physician who prances around our hospital in a Halloween costume?"

I groaned and threw my hands up in the air. "Like I said before, this is all crazy! How could anyone possibly fake an operation? I know you must have it on videotape."

The doctor walked toward me again. "Mr. Green, haven't you ever watched some of the medical dramas on TV?"

"Not really."

"Haven't you ever seen any episodes of *Grey's Anatomy*?"

"No."

"What about *Scrubs*?"

"No."

"*The Good Doctor*?"

"No."

"*Nip / Tuck*?"

25

"No."

"*Nurse Jackie?*"

"No."

"*The Knick?*"

"No."

"*ER?*"

"No."

"*General Hospital?*"

"No."

"*Casualty?*"

"No."

"*Chicago Med?*"

"No."

"*Nurses?*"

"No."

"*New Amsterdam?*"

"No."

"*The Resident?*"

"No."

"*Doogie Howser MD?*"

"No."

"*House?*"

"Uh, yes...I did see a couple episodes of *House.*"

"Well then tell me, Mr. Green, how do you suppose they manage to film all those realistic-looking operations for TV? Do you think they go up to sick people and say 'Hi, do you mind if we cut you open so millions can see your insides on TV?'"

"That's probably not how they do it."

"You're right, Mr. Green. But I *do* know how they do it. They use cow organs, chicken fat, and a lot of Halloween blood."

Dr. Dred punched up her cell phone once again. "Janet, I want you to call the county morgue and ask them if they're missing any cadavers or cadaver spines...and check with our medical teaching college here on campus and ask them the same thing."

"Yes, ma'am."

The doctor covered the phone with one hand and whispered to me, "I'll call every funeral home in Columbus if I have to, Mr. Green."

"Oh, and Janet…I also want you to call our west campus farm and ask them if they're missing any cows."

"Missing cows?"

"Is there an echo on this line, Janet?"

"No, ma'am, I'll get on it right away."

The doctor hung up her phone and looked at me. "So if we know that the spinal surgery was faked, then we'd also have to assume that *all* of Carli's injuries were faked. Wouldn't you agree, Mr. Green? Oh, don't answer that… I know you've got your Fifth Amendment rights. By the way, would you like to 'lawyer up' now?"

I exhaled deeply. "No, because this is the stupidest line of questioning I've ever heard in my life."

"It sounds like you agree with me then…that her injuries *were* faked. Hollywood must have been working overtime on *this* patient."

Then the doctor began pacing back and forth in front of the x-rays. "Let's try working this backwards," she said. "Who were the people handling Carli before the surgery? You had the paramedics in the ambulance, the ER staff here at the hospital, and my ICU staff. But who on my own staff would want to undermine me? I'll bet it was Jessica. She thinks I'm an ogre."

"I can't imagine why."

"Don't flatter me, Mr. Green. Your daughter worked in that sandwich shop across the street from the hospital. Is that correct?"

"Yes."

"So she had access to speak privately with every member of this facility… bypassing any possibility that cell phone records could be traced. I think that the pieces of this puzzle are finally starting to fall into place, Mr. Green. Are you getting nervous?"

I sighed. "No, just more annoyed."

"Well, it had to be an inside job," she continued. "No matter how good Hollywood pieced her together, there should have been someone along the chain who should have recognized something wasn't right. My only question on that is just how many 'moles' did you have assisting you in the operation?"

"Operation?"

"The *hoax*, Mr. Green…Pay attention. So the paramedics who were first on the scene had to be crooked. They had to make sure that Carli's makeup was perfectly in place, so that she looked gory enough to pass muster with a large crowd gawking at her nearby."

Dr. Dred stopped talking. She then paced slowly around the large meeting room tables for several minutes looking downward in thought.

I finally stood up and demanded, "Can I go now?"

"Sit down!" she snapped back. "There's still one thing that really bothers me…If Carli's injuries had to be faked, then why did her husband's injuries have to be real? This picture is starting to look extremely ugly, Mr. Green."

I sat back down and said, "You just keep making up all these psycho accusations without a shred of evidence."

"Oh, we have all the evidence we need, Mr. Green. What we need now is the truth. Did your daughter have any boyfriends on the side? Had she been having arguments with her husband?"

"How would I know?"

The doctor then spoke very loudly. "Because the truth is…that you and Carli concocted this entire hoax as a diversion to cover up the MURDER of her husband, Marty Newman!"

"NO! THAT'S CRAZY!" I cried out.

"The fire was arson!"

"NO!"

"Carli wasn't even upstairs when the fire broke out. She never jumped out of the second-story window!"

"NO!"

"And she let the dogs die to garner more public sympathy. Isn't that right, Mr. Green?"

"NO!"

"And as I recall, Carli's first words after the accident weren't 'Is Marty okay?' No, she wanted to know if Marty was DEAD! The only thing she cared about was making sure that the plan was a success."

My voice was weak now. "I don't know," I mumbled in exhaustion.

"So you've switched your story now from 'no' to 'I don't know'? It didn't take me that long to crack this case now, did it? The girl walks away from all this as the miracle heroine while her husband dies. We'll have to check and see if Ohio has any family-friendly prisons where you and your daughter can share adjacent cells."

My eyes looked up. "Dr. Dred, what did you mean by 'miracle heroine'?"

The doctor ignored my question. "Put the cuffs on now, Mr. Green," she ordered.

"You're not a policeman."

"Put the cuffs on now in front!" she yelled. "Or I'll have one of these fine gentlemen with a badge attach them behind your back and it won't be quite as comfortable."

I did as ordered. I didn't want her to see the tear coming down from my left eye. "Are you going to water-board me too?" I asked sarcastically.

"If that would loosen your tongue, then I'm sure we could make the arrangements."

Then she stood behind me. I thought she would dig her nails in, but instead, she started breathing down my neck with her nose again. Why was this woman so creepy?

Then she shifted just a little, and I could feel her lips grazing my right ear. She whispered, "Look at how the little man squirms as the truth comes out."

SEVEN

The head of ICU seemed quite pleased with her work. "Hoaxer number one down…hoaxer number two coming up. Sit back and watch the show, Mr. Green."

She affixed Carli's x-rays back on the light board, and then punched up her cell phone. "Hello, Dr. Duncan? Yes, that code yellow we had was one of *your* patients. Can you come up to my conference room please?…Good, thanks."

"Oh, and try to look surprised, Mr. Green."

The crocodile-hunting physician entered shortly and cast a skewed glance at the gentleman in manacles. "Out drunk last night? Eh, mate?"

Then he turned to Dr. Dred. "So you say one of my patients was a runner?"

"Well, at first, we thought she was a kidnap victim, but such was not the case. Take a look at Carli Green's two x-rays, Doctor. See if you notice anything unusual."

The surgeon's eyes darted back and forth between the two images and he concluded, "The only thing unusual is…this is some of my best work."

"It should be," answered Dr. Dred, "especially if you were working on a cadaver."

The surgeon's eyes nearly bulged out of their sockets, and he pointed an index finger at his counterpart. "You watch your tongue, Doctor," he hissed. "If you do anything to sully my reputation, I'll have you drummed out of this hospital faster than I can skin a red-bellied black snake."

"I don't bow to your threats, Dr. Duncan. The fact is that your patient doesn't look anything like those x-rays."

The man's voice roared back. "And just WHAT are you implying, Doctor?!"

With an equal roar, the woman bellowed, "I'm implying that you either DELIBERATELY performed a nine-hour surgery on a cadaver spine…or—"

"Or WHAT?"

"Or…you were duped."

With lightning quickness, Dr. Duncan reached into his lab coat and hurled his foot-long, razor-sharp stainless steel hunting knife across the room and lodged it into the wall above Dr. Dred's head.

He calmly said, "I missed on purpose, love. Next time I won't."

Seeing the two doctors nearly kill each other, I realized that there was no point watching hospital dramas on TV because I was now in one myself. The two officers quickly approached Dr. Duncan, but Dr. Dred put up a stop sign with her hand.

"Let it go," she told them. "It's just a game he likes to play."

There was a quick knock at the door and this time, a long line of men and women began filing into the conference room. The first gentleman looked quite distinguished in his perfectly fitted suit. It was complemented by a balding head, gray on the side, and a gray closely trimmed beard.

He walked directly over to my side of the table arrangement and sat down next to me, offering his hand to my manacled wrists. "Hello, I'm Dr. Barrington Stanton, Chairman of the Board of The Ohio State University Medical Center. These other folks are members of the board of directors and we also have four agents from the FBI."

"Roland Green," I replied, "but I'm not sure why you would want to shake my hand."

"You're the only one here in handcuffs," he remarked, "so you must be very important."

Dr. Stanton stood back up and turned around. He dislodged the hunting knife from the wall and offered it back to its owner. "Target practice, Dr. Duncan?" he mused.

"Sorry, sir, it slipped…won't happen again."

Drs. Dred and Duncan stood as the chairman pointed at me.

"Dr. Dred, why is this man wearing handcuffs?"

Dr. Dred stepped forward and pointed an accusatory finger at me. "Dr. Stanton, I've already solved the case. Seated next to you now is the most diabolically clever criminal mastermind in the history of medical science."

The chairman rolled his eyes and retorted, "Really? Well, thank you, Clarise…It isn't every day that Hannibal Lecter falls into our lap."

There was a brief murmur of chuckling in the room as the chairman pointed to one of the uniformed officers. "Key please."

It felt good to have my handcuffs removed and I sensed that an atmosphere of sanity was making a comeback.

The chairman continued. "Dr. Dred, when I heard that you initiated a total lockdown of this facility, followed by the appearance of the FBI at my door, I suspected that something was seriously afoot at ICU. Would you care to explain?"

31

"I'd be more than happy to, Mr. Chairman," she replied. "I take full responsibility for everything that's happened today…AND for cracking the case."

"What case?" the chairman responded.

"Sir, Mr. Green, here, and his daughter attempted to perpetrate a monstrous hoax against this hospital designed to portray Miss Green as a 'miracle heroine' while at the same time, covering up the murder of her husband, Marty Newman. I'm the one who sniffed out the scheme, I cuffed the father, and I put the daughter behind bars."

The chairman slapped the palm of his hand down so hard on the table that all four tables shook. "Dr. Dred, STOP IT!" he blustered. "This investigation will be conducted thoroughly and professionally. There will be no rush to judgment."

"Yes, sir."

"And what do you mean, you put the daughter behind bars?"

"I sent officers to escort her to a room on the eighth floor. And don't worry, our record is unblemished. There's never been an escape."

"And why on earth would you put a burn patient in the prison ward?"

"Because she's *not* a burn patient. She a fake, a fraud, a cheat, a rogue, a phony, a hoaxer, a menace, a scoundrel, a bluffer, a shyster, a trickster, a charlatan, a conniver, a beguiler, an imposter, a con artist, a deceiver, a hypocrite, a pretender, a fugitive, a desperado, a reprobate, a scalawag, a flummoxer, a four-flusher, a flimflammer, a hood-winker, a hornswoggler, a bumfuzzler—"

"That's enough, Doctor!" the chairman ordered. "Before this conversation goes any further, I want every person in this room to follow me to the eighth floor and we will meet Miss Green in person."

Finally, before this day got any crazier, I would get to see my daughter. Our large group went up in two elevators and we arrived at what was commonly referred to as the "naughty ward." But it was not a pleasant entry. I could already recognize Carli's voice, screaming in terror and crying…somewhere down the hallway.

"Wow," I thought. "The rooms really do have bars."

When we arrived at Carli's cell, my wife, Laura, was also in tears. She huddled closely with Carli and had her covered with a blanket. They were both sitting up on the bed.

Between her weeping, Laura said, "The inmates have been screaming profanities at us since the moment we got here."

Dr. Stanton took charge immediately. "LISTEN UP, YOU IDIOTS!" he bellowed down the hallway. "The next inmate who says a disparaging word to this young woman will get zero rations for the next twenty-four hours! Do I make myself clear?"

The "naughty ward" fell silent.

Dr. Stanton mumbled to me, "That's illegal, of course, but the inmates don't know it."

Then he shook his head at the leader of ICU. "Dr. Dred…what were you thinking?"

"Sir…I—"

"I don't want to hear it, Doctor. As soon as we get done in this cell, I'm putting you and your staff in charge of caring for Carli and her mom. Get them a nice room, feed them dinner, and for God's sake, get the young lady some decent clothes. Go out and buy them if you have to."

"Yes, sir."

Dr. Stanton tapped my shoulder. "Mr. Green, would you follow me into the cell, please?"

"Hello, Miss Carli," he said gently. "I'm Dr. Stanton, the chairman of the hospital. We're going to get you out of this place as soon as possible, but first I have to take a quick peek at your back. Would you be willing to let me do that?"

Carli sniffed through a tissue and nodded. Then Dr. Stanton slowly lowered the cloth that was covering her back.

I began hyperventilating. I just could not comprehend what I was looking at. The horror of second and third degree burns that earlier would make me gag was now simply not there…gone…vanished. I saw now only smooth, healthy skin and I wanted to hug her so badly, but I stood back, afraid to jinx such good fortune. I thought about the wonderment of the Navajo healing ceremony and I didn't care that what Rising Sun had done was physically impossible. Right now, I trusted my eyes.

Dr. Stanton made the official call to the group behind us. "Confirming… the patient Carli Green has no burn wounds."

It was followed by a lot of confused murmuring in the group. Then he turned to his aide and instructed, "Ryan, grab me one of the portable x-ray machines, please…the AirTouch."

"Yes, sir."

I didn't even know that such an advanced gadget existed. It looked somewhat like a large digital camera…or a laptop with a camera lens jutting out.

Dr. Stanton placed it as to snap a picture of Carli's spine from a side angle. The x-ray immediately popped up on the laptop screen.

"Confirming," the doctor called out, "the patient Carli Green has no titanium rods or screws in her spine. Ryan, we need a plastic printout of this x-ray."

The crocodile hunter pointed at the picture. "Well that proves this whole thing is a hoax…the hoax of the century."

Dr. Dred glared right at Duncan and asked, "But who all is *involved* in this hoax?"

Dr. Stanton snapped at them, "Doctors, once again, we will not rush to judgment. For now, keep your opinions to yourself."

Dr. Duncan, feeling his personal reputation on the line, queried, "Are we just going to glance over the possibility of a twin or a clone?"

"She has no twin, Duncan," Dr. Dred sneered, "and a clone is crazy."

"Not as crazy as you, love."

"Enough now, Doctors," the chairman admonished them. "Mrs. Green, can you think of a question that only you and your daughter would know the answer to?"

My wife thought it over for a few seconds and then asked, "Carli, when you were little, do you remember who gave you 'the talk'…you know, the birds and the bees…Was it Mom or Dad?"

Our daughter responded quickly, "It was Dad."

"And do you remember what you said to me when it was done?"

"I said, 'I don't want to have a period.'"

Laura looked back at Dr. Stanton and stated, "This is my daughter."

"Mrs. Green, thank you. Miss Carli, you've been a wonderful patient and I apologize for today's hardships. You'll be moved to a nice guest room now. Mr. Green, you're still with me."

"Yes, sir."

"Everyone, let's get back to the conference room."

I finally felt comfortable enough to kiss both my wife and my daughter a temporary goodbye. "Spirits up, stay strong," I urged them.

When we returned to the conference room, Ryan had already clipped x-ray number three to the light board.

"Dr. Duncan," said the chairman, "you're in the spotlight now. Take a look at the three x-rays…pre-op, post-op, and today…and tell us what you see…and please use a normal pointer, not your crocodile spear."

The surgeon walked up to the light board and his eyes darted back and forth for several minutes…1,2,3…3,2,1…1,3…2,3…1,2…2,3…2,3…2,3… Then he stopped and cleared his throat.

"Um…we seem to have a bit of a conundrum here."

"How so?" asked the chairman.

"Well the x-rays are definitely from the same person. You can see the micro-fissures are identical on each spine segment and so are the segment shapes. Every human applies a different wear-and-tear pattern to their spine as they go through life. So even identical twins would have different spinal patterns. They're unique, like fingerprints. And that proves that the surgery was performed on Carli's real spine and not on a cadaver. Sorry, Dr. Dred. I just blew your theory clean out of the water."

"Is that all?" asked Dr. Stanton.

"Oh, no. The real problem is with x-ray three. If I were Rod Serling, this is where I'd cue up the *Twilight Zone* theme. Not only are the rods and screws gone, but the L2 segment has poofed up back to normal. Carli needed the surgery for a compressed L2. If you compress a marshmallow, it might regain its original shape, but crushed bone can not be un-crushed. So the change from x-ray two to x-ray three is contrary to reason…even though we're looking at it."

The center speakerphone rang. "Dr. Dred, this is Janet. The West Campus Farm reports that they have no missing cows."

Dr. Dred regretted the poor timing of the announcement. "Thank you, Janet."

The chairman raised an eyebrow. "Dr. Dred, did you find a lost cow?" More reserved chuckling followed from the group.

"No, sir."

"Did one follow you home?"

"No, sir. It's a fact that most fake operations for TV shows use cow organs to make them look authentic. I was just doing my due diligence, sir."

"Or perhaps over-doing your diligence? Dr. Dred, do you have anything to add to Dr. Duncan's analysis?"

"I have a *lot* to add, sir. For one, this investigation must stop in its tracks and turn its focus to the key piece of evidence in the case…and that's Mr. Green's Navajo Event."

"What exactly is a Navajo Event?" the chairman asked.

"It's a poorly thought out caper involving five co-conspirators who participated in the hoax. Mr. Green hired his cousin, Dr. Bill Green, and four alleged Navajos to perform an alleged healing ceremony on Carli, and then allegedly turned her into the "miracle heroine" that the world would fawn over while at the same time using the miracle as a convenient cover-up for the murder of her husband, Marty Newman."

"Whoa!...Whoa!...Whoa!" the chairman called out. "Dr. Dred, those are some extremely serious charges and I'm sure if there's any validity to them, these four FBI agents will take the time to listen to you. But we are NOT running the Salem witch trials here and I strongly urge you to use caution before uttering any more public accusations. You could get sued. Our whole facility could get sued...and your career would be over."

"Yes, sir. I'll try to be more careful, sir."

The chairman turned in my direction and said, "Mr. Green, the ball's in your court. Please enlighten us if you can. Tell us your version of the Navajo Event."

With the chairman at my side, I felt emboldened to speak my mind. I stood and said calmly, "Dr. Dred is full of horse manure."

That got the biggest laugh of the day, but I didn't say it to be funny. It was the truth.

"Five years ago, my family visited these same people at their home on the Navajo Reservation. For such a short visit, we developed close ties. My cousin, Dr. Bill Green, has been their physician for many years. My wife and I were certainly not expecting their visit in the ICU. The very old medicine man, Rising Sun, had come here specifically to perform a healing ceremony for Carli. Well, apparently it worked, and we're all shocked by the good results."

"Would you call this a miracle, Mr. Green?" asked the chairman.

"I don't know the definition of a miracle. What I witnessed was a healing ceremony that healed."

"Can you describe this ceremony in detail, Mr. Green?"

"I tried to with Dr. Dred, but she put me in handcuffs. The problem is that my words aren't adequate to describe what I saw."

"Just give it a try," the chairman urged.

"Well, the women sang and shook the gourd rattle, the boy beat his drum, and Rising Sun kept his hands over his heart...and then the three... what should I call them? I'll call them the 'physical stimuli.'"

"Explain."

"Well, first there was some bright light over Carli's body, then some water droplets, then weird stuff that looked like Fourth of July sparklers. The whole thing was over in less than ten minutes."

Dr. Stanton leaned back in his chair. "Mr. Green, how were the physical stimuli created?"

"I have no clue…I thought they were just magic tricks."

"*That's* an idea," the chairman thought out loud. "Professional magicians are the one group who would be most qualified to unravel this mystery and get us answers. If they're good, they should be able to re-create it and solve the puzzle."

Dr. Stanton pointed to his aide. "Ryan, I want you to get on the phone and call as many great professional magicians as you can and tell them they need to fly to Columbus tomorrow. We'll pay their airfare and don't hesitate to call the big names either…David Copperfield…Penn and Teller…Murray SawChuck…Call everybody. Tell them that their prestige would go through the roof if they could be the first ones to solve the world's greatest medical hoax…The Navajo Event."

The chairman checked his watch. "Before we close up shop for the day, I want to give some homework assignments to our FBI friends. Mr. Zimblist, first thing we need are DNA samples. I want you and your crew to collect samples from everywhere Carli's been…her apartment, the paramedics, the emergency room, the ICU, the spinal surgery O.R., and a current blood sample. Okay? See if they all match."

"Next…Mr. Green. Would you be willing to take a lie-detector test? You know, a polygraph?"

That was easy. I put both outstretched arms on the table and announced, "Let's do it."

"Well, not just you, Mr. Green. I want every employee in this hospital who's had any contact with Carli this week to take one too. And that includes you also, Dr. Dred and Dr. Duncan."

Dr. Dred looked none too pleased. She asked, "What if someone on my staff refuses to take the polygraph?"

"Then hand them their final paycheck. If there are no other questions, then we'll all meet back here at 10:00 a.m. tomorrow."

"Wait!" Dr. Dred called out, while raising a hand. "The Greens are still suspects in a crime. They're a flight risk. Shouldn't they be locked up overnight?"

Dr. Stanton turned to me. "Mr. Green, would you give me your word that you and your family will not try to flee?"

"Absolutely," I responded.

"And Dr. Dred…would you give me *your* word that *you* won't try to flee?"

I thought, "Wow, I really like this guy, Stanton." But I especially enjoyed the priceless, twisted expression of outrage on the doctor's face.

Her fury was evident when she called to the surgeon, "Hey, Duncan, let me borrow your 'pointer.'"

"Sorry, love," he replied, "but I don't trust your aim."

EIGHT

The room we had been assigned was like a nice hotel room. I didn't even realize that a hospital could have such nice accommodations unrelated to the medical side of business. We woke at 7:00 a.m., the seventh day since our arrival, and turned on the *Today* show to catch up on the news…but were totally unprepared for the shock.

"Breaking news as we come on the air this morning…A Columbus, Ohio woman is being dubbed the 'miracle girl' after reportedly being completely healed by a Navajo medicine man after she had suffered horrific burns in an apartment fire in which her husband had perished. Twenty-one-year-old Carli Green was recovering from burn wounds and a broken spine at The Ohio State University Medical Center when she received a surprise visit from four members of the Navajo Nation."

I grabbed the TV remote and turned up the volume.

"We are told that they performed a brief healing ceremony and then quickly departed. The incident, now being referred to as the Navajo Event, has captured the imaginations of people around the globe. As we speak, hordes of news crews are descending upon the hospital seeking more information and a chance to perhaps interview the young woman. But keep in mind that others are calling it a monstrous hoax designed just to grab attention and are comparing it to the infamous 'Balloon Boy' hoax of 2009."

The three of us looked at each other, but said nothing. We went to the curtains of our south-facing window above the hospital's main entrance and drew them open. We could scarcely believe what we saw. There were hundreds, perhaps thousands of news crew trucks packed tightly in the hospital's driveway and backed up as far as our eyes could see.

I muttered, "Now we sure know how the President of the United States feels when someone leaks a story."

We took the elevator to the basement food court to get breakfast and fortunately, our photos had not yet been splattered across the TV screens. We knew that would change. But for now, no one paid us the slightest bit of attention. Afterward, we thought it best for Laura and Carli to stay in the hotel room while I returned to the conference room at the requested 10:00 a.m. hour.

The same people I had met yesterday were gathering in their seats as coffee was being served.

"Thank you for arriving punctually," began Dr. Stanton. "I apologize for the insanity at our front doors this morning but, nonetheless, we have a lot of work to do."

The chairman's aide noted, "Sir, members of the news media are asking us for a statement."

"Ryan, there will be no statements until our investigation is completed. Today, I'd like the FBI to continue collecting DNA samples and administering polygraphs to our staff...anyone who worked with Carli...and don't forget to locate those two paramedics who brought her to the hospital. Ryan, were you able to contact any professional magicians?"

"Yes, sir. Six have accepted our invitation and are on their way now."

"Excellent, and what about the Columbus Fire Marshal?"

The meeting was suddenly interrupted by several chimes from the speakerphone. "Dr. Stanton, you have the pope on line three."

The chairman spoke gruffly. "I'm not in the mood for games, Janet."

"Oh, no sir...We called back the Vatican to be sure and they put the pope on the line. It's the real deal, sir."

Dr. Stanton looked around the room. "Well, this is a first. Assuming it's the real pope, does anyone know how I would address him? Is it something like 'Your Excellency'?"

One of the board members noted, "That would be more appropriate for a bishop. For the pope, I suggest you try 'Your Holiness.'"

"Thank you. Let's all try to be quiet now."

The chairman took a deep breath and pressed line three, speaking loudly and clearly. "Your Holiness, this is Dr. Barrington Stanton, chairman of The Ohio State University Medical Center. We are greatly honored by your unexpected greeting. How may we be of service?"

In contrast, the pontiff began his address quietly. "Good morning, Dr. Stanton. It is my understanding that a miracle *may* have taken place at your facility this week."

"Your Holiness, we are currently in the midst of a detailed investigation into that possibility and as yet, no conclusion has been drawn."

"Dr. Stanton, we here at the Vatican take our miracles very seriously."

"That's quite understandable, Your Holiness."

"Many people assume that our enclave is populated only by the devoutly religious. But we also employ people whom I like to refer to as my 'skeptics.' These are world-renowned scientists whose main occupation is to prove or disprove miracles."

"You are correct, Your Holiness. I did not know this."

"Dr. Stanton, I would be most indebted to your generosity if you would permit four of my scientific emissaries to monitor your evidence gathering as you move forward in this investigation. Rest assured these individuals will not interfere. They are sworn to secrecy and report back only to myself. They will not contribute an iota to the ongoing news chaos."

"I see. Please allow me a moment to consult with my board."

"Of course."

The chairman placed line three on hold. "Gentlemen, this is a bit irregular but I'm okay with it if you are. In fact, if these people have experience digging into this type of phenomena, they might even be able to help us find the answers we're looking for. Do I have any objections?…No?…Then it's settled."

"Your Holiness, we would be greatly honored to have your scientific emissaries join us. How soon can they get here?"

"Soon," answered the pontiff. "Thank you and goodbye."

As the line went dead, there was a knock at the conference door and four emissaries entered the room wearing western-style suits and ties and took seats around the table on their own, leaving everyone's jaw agape.

Only one of the men spoke. "Good morning, my good friends. I am Monsignor Mateo Romano. Did His Holiness mention that we take our miracles very seriously?"

"He most certainly did," replied the chairman, shaking his head.

Then, once again, the meeting was interrupted by the chimes of the speakerphone. "Dr. Stanton, you have a visitor."

"Janet, right now, I would be none too surprised if Jesus himself walked through our door."

"No, sir…It's the Columbus Fire Marshal."

"Close enough. Send him in."

I looked forward to seeing this man again, who had come to visit Carli in the ICU. He once more wore his full dress uniform and he placed his hat on the first table. If any public servant could display a compassionate face, it was this man…gray, bespectacled, but young looking. And he carried two objects in his right hand.

"Edward Barnes, fire marshal," he quickly introduced himself. "I've been asked to come here today to present my analysis of the Green / Newman fire in east Columbus."

The fire marshal got right down to business. He was not interested in knowing the names of the people in the room.

"Based on the burn patterns in the stairway, we know for certain that the fire originated at the base of the sofa in the living room. We see this type of fire all the time. The electric lamp cord I'm holding accidentally got stuck under the metal castor of the sofa leg that I'm showing you now. The castor pattern matches the wear marks on the cord. After months of people sitting, the castor wore away the plastic coating over the wires, and once the two wires touch, you get a rather nasty explosion, which usually sets off a fire."

Dr. Dred raised her hand. "Mr. Barnes, is it possible that this fire could have been caused by arson?"

"Ma'am, it's not unusual for appliances like toasters to be used to set off electrical fires. In this case, however, an arsonist would have had to plop himself on the sofa about five hundred times to match the wear pattern on the cord. So no, I highly doubt this was arson."

When I heard that, I let out a deep sigh and whispered to myself, "Thank you, Mr. Barnes."

"Moving on, the fire quickly shot up the staircase and set off the smoke alarm…and we're talking about seconds here, not minutes. We know that Carli awoke and opened the front window, but that gave oxygen to the fire and created a backdraft. There's no actual flame in a backdraft, but the super-heated air will move across the ceiling at a temperature of about a thousand degrees Fahrenheit. Where she stood, the air roasted her back and the back of her arms for about a tenth of a second at six hundred degrees. It looks like a sunburn across the entire area except for the line that was covered by her bra strap. But the skin damage goes deep. I visited the young woman in the ICU. She's a real trooper."

"Finishing up, they both exited out the twelve-foot second story window. The woman landed on grass and sustained a compression fracture of the spine along with a broken ankle. The husband, unfortunately, landed on the sidewalk and did not survive."

Dr. Dred raised her hand again. "I'm sorry I have to ask this, Mr. Barnes, but is there any possible way that the woman could have remained on the first floor and faked her injuries?"

"You're sorry?" asked the fire marshal. "You ought to be. You don't like the young lady, do you? As the head of ICU, Dr. Dred, surely you've seen many, many burn patients come through your ward. Is this not true?"

"It is."

"And with all those years of experience, do you consider yourself capable of discerning a real burn wound from a fake one?"

"I believe I am."

"Then why are you asking me?"

Dr. Stanton jumped to his feet to break up an extremely awkward moment. "Thank you very much for your insight, Mr. Barnes. Let's all now break for lunch."

Before he could exit the room, the fire marshal was flagged down by Monsignor Romano, one of the pope's emissaries. "Mr. Barnes, can you please look at x-ray three. The compression fracture you spoke of is no longer present. The metal parts from her surgery have also vanished. And we are told that she now has perfectly smooth skin."

"Yes, I've heard the news reports."

The emissary pressed on. "We have observed that you are a man of great wisdom and stature in the United States. Can you tell me please, in your opinion, if you believe these are miracles?"

The fire marshal sighed. "Sir, I'm afraid that's really not my department. I usually leave it to the man upstairs."

"Yes, of course. Can you please tell me the name of this man upstairs?"

"Uh…God?"

NINE

The chairman had lunch catered in, so it was convenient not to have to leave the conference room. The hour was spent in idle chit-chat discussing the Buckeyes' chances of winning the Big Ten football title this year. Though there was a TV in the room, he had no intention of turning on the news.

At 1:00 p.m., Dr. Stanton called our meeting back to order. "While the FBI continues its fieldwork, I'd like us to return to examining the details of the Navajo Event. Mr. Green has already given us his version and he was the only witness. So if we can, I'd like to talk to the principals. Mr. Green, do you think that the medicine man, Rising Sun, would be willing to speak with us?"

"Honestly, sir, if Rising Sun is watching the news today, I would think he would want to be left alone."

"I see. Well, what about your cousin, the physician? Would Dr. Bill Green be willing to share his thoughts and insights?"

"It's possible. We could try calling him." I fumbled for my wallet and pulled out my cousin's business card. "Do you want me to go ahead?"

"Yes, please. Use the speakerphone, but let me do the talking."

I punched up his number and waited through four rings.

"Dr. Green," he answered.

"Good afternoon, Dr. Green. This is Dr. Barrington Stanton, chairman of The Ohio State University Medical Center. How are you today, sir?"

"Fine, thank you."

"Dr. Green, first I want to apologize for all the commotion going on in the news media. This is certainly not what we wanted nor expected."

"No need for an apology, Doctor. It was our choice to fly to Columbus. And by the way, your campus airport is a nice facility."

"Well, thank you for that, Dr. Green. I know this may be asking a lot, but would it be at all possible for us to speak to your medicine man, Rising Sun? All courtesy and respect would be given."

"I'm afraid that won't be possible, Dr. Stanton."

"May I ask why not?"

"Because Rising Sun has entered the fourth world. He's dead."

"NOOOOOOOOOOOOOOOOOO!" I can't remember ever allowing myself to scream so loudly. I pounded my fist on the table until my hand hurt. Then I got up and started walking in circles around the room, passing behind the back of every member of the group.

"This is all MY fault!" I yelled at the speaker phone.

"Roland, no!" my cousin yelled back. "If you're not already seated, then please sit down now."

"Ohhhhhhhhhhh," I moaned, and rested my head on the table top.

"Roland," he said again. "Take a deep breath. There are things that I need to explain."

I did as told and took several deep breaths in an attempt to calm myself down.

"Roland, Rising Sun was very aware that his remaining days on this earth were few. And he wanted to go out with—"

"With a bang," I filled in my cousin's words.

"No, he said he wanted to go out with a good deed. And I told him that my Jewish people refer to this as a 'mitzvah.'"

"How did Rising Sun react to that?"

"Well, I was quite taken aback when he slapped my knee and said, 'Yes... we must do a mitzvah.' And this was just a few days before Carli's accident. The timing was most fortuitous."

"Dr. Green," the chairman interrupted. "This story is quite amazing and I know that all of us here feel blessed that Rising Sun was able to come to our facility to fulfill his final quest."

Bill paused, then asked, "Wait, are you saying the news reports are true... that the healing ceremony worked?"

This time, I was the one who interrupted. "Bill, please tell the Navajo Nation that he succeeded...spectacularly."

"I'm sure the Nation will be very pleased to hear that, Roland."

The chairman resumed control of the conversation. "Dr. Green, the real reason for our call is to learn more about the healing ceremony itself, that is, if you are willing to share what you know."

"Certainly, and I've studied the ceremony for years. But you have to keep in mind that it's like asking an astronomer to tell us everything he knows about the universe. There's so much more that he does *not* know."

"Yes, of course, but anything you can tell us would be helpful. Your cousin Roland referred to three physical stimuli...light, water, and sparklers, but he just thought they were magic tricks."

"Is *that* how he described them?" Bill noted with an amused chuckle. "I'm pretty sure I can do a little better than that. The bright light, for one, is not a solid wall of light. Think of it more as a million laser pens all pointing in the same direction, and packed together so tightly that they appear to be one powerful searchlight. Now, the human body has about 35 trillion cells. The light beams pass between the cells in straight lines throughout the entire body, and create kind of a superhighway for the coming mist, or water droplets."

"But Dr. Green, how do you know this?" asked the chairman.

"Some of the stories are passed down through generations of medicine men. What I try to do is interpret the stories in such a manner that they would be consistent with science and physics…even if today's scientists are not capable of duplicating the observed phenomena."

"So you're saying that Rising Sun would just attribute his success to…let's say, the Great Spirit…or God as we call him?"

"Essentially, that's correct, but the supreme beings here are referred to as DIYIN DiNé'E, the holy people. There's more than one god."

"Thank you. Okay, then what's going on in phase two, the water? What is that all about?"

"Each phase becomes more complex, so what I'm telling you is my best guess. It's not water like we know it. In fact if you were to touch it, it wouldn't even feel wet because each water molecule is separate from all the others. This is a big number, but a single drop of water contains 1.5 sextillion water molecules, each with the familiar composition H2O. Visually, it looks a bit like the spray mists they use on grocery store veggies. But chemically, individual water molecules exist as a gas. Do you want me to keep going?"

"Yes, Dr. Green. Please continue."

"I will, but you have to understand that this type of physics doesn't happen in the ordinary world that you and I know."

"I hear you, Dr. Green. But right now, your best guess is better than anything else we've got going."

"Okay…Those water molecules follow the paths created by the light and integrate with the molecules of bad cells or any foreign substance, thereby breaking them up. This can happen even with the hardest metals. Individual H2O molecules can stick to almost any other substance. So those individual bad and foreign molecules break off from their group and either evaporate or recede with the water. What I haven't been able to figure out is how the water molecules know which materials are foreign objects or bad cells like burns or cancer…and which are good human cells, which are left alone."

"What you're saying is impossible."

"Roland and I say that all the time too. But, here, take this example…If

46

someone gives you a five-hundred-sheet ream of paper and asks you to tear it in half, you can't do it. But…if you run each sheet through a shredder, then your mound of confetti is quite easy to divide in half. You can even pour it out almost like a liquid."

"And the sparklers?"

"It's nothing at all like sparklers…It's more, uh…I guess what I want to call it is a box of atoms…like a kid's chemistry set that contains samples of every element on the periodic table. When you see it swirling around over a person's body, it might resemble something like the transporter on *Star Trek*…energy particles…beam me up Scotty, that sort of thing. Maybe that's why Roland called it sparklers."

"But what does it do?"

"It does the hard part…the 'heavy lifting,' so to speak. I won't pretend to understand it myself, but it works like a chef following a recipe and that recipe is, of course, DNA."

"Building blocks."

"Yes, exactly. In our *Star Trek* example, the transporter has to reassemble 6.5 octillion atoms in absolute perfect order to recreate the original person. When the swirl of atoms reached Carli's compressed L2 vertebra segment, it created, from the DNA map, the proper amount of bone matter…calcium, phosphorous, oxygen, and hydrogen…to rebuild that segment back to its original healthy state."

"But how were the burns treated?"

"Same as bone…except instead of calcium, skin contains carbon and nitrogen. Third-degree burns penetrate all three layers of the skin…the epidermis, the dermis, and the hypodermis. The mist washes away damaged skin from all three layers, and the energy particles rebuild healthy, normal skin."

"Dr. Green, do you really believe that Rising Sun healed Carli?"

"Certainly."

"But why?"

"Because I witnessed the healing ceremony on seven previous occasions. I used to think that he was just a faith healer. He was curing some big-ticket items like cancer, diabetes, pulmonary disease, and tumors…but these are diseases that, although rare, can sometimes go away on their own. But then there was Little Bear, a thirteen-year-old boy whose arms were cut off in a farming accident. With my own eyes, I watched Rising Sun re-attach his arms without so much as touching the boy."

"More amazement. So if the tribe had this medicine man, why did they need you?"

"The healing ceremony took a lot out of Rising Sun. He needed several days to recover after each two-hour performance. Yesterday, however, it was sped up, and he did not recover."

"Well, that explains to the critics why he couldn't go from room to room healing everyone. Dr. Green, we owe you a great deal of gratitude for enlightening us on the subject matter. And please pass along our deepest condolences to the Navajo Nation."

"I certainly will."

"Goodbye."

Dr. Stanton hung up the phone. "Okay, everyone, that was a very good conversation. We're going to retire for the day now and meet back again at 10:00 a.m. tomorrow. I've issued a gag order to all employees. No one is to talk to the media about the Navajo Event until after my news conference which will most likely occur tomorrow. Thank you all."

* * *

We decided to order hospital food trays for dinner in our room. It actually tasted pretty good for hospital food, and we didn't want to go down to the food court again. I asked Laura and Carli if we should dare turn on the 6:30 p.m. national news. Curiosity got the best of us.

"Good evening. This is a Special Report from ABC News. We are here in Columbus, Ohio tonight with a story that is causing worldwide hysteria and has come to be known as the Navajo Event. Twenty-one-year-old Carli Green, who last week suffered massive injuries in an apartment fire that killed her husband, has reportedly been completely healed by a visiting Navajo medicine man known as Rising Sun."

Laura and I looked at each other. I said, "Worldwide hysteria? That's cool, but even more importantly, how are your mashed potatoes and green beans?"

The TV blared, "As you can see behind me, a crowd estimated to number about fifty thousand has gathered in front of The Ohio State University Medical Center in hopes of seeing, or perhaps even touching a woman that many here say has been touched by God."

"Sorry," I told the TV, "but *we* reserve that privilege." Laura and I both gave Carli a big squeeze that finally got her to smile.

"And, Daniel," added the reporter, "they're all hoping that a little bit of

Carli Green's *mojo* might rub off on them."

The news anchor queried, "Roberta, have hospital administrators or the Greens themselves made any kind of statement yet?"

"No, Daniel, but we're expecting to hear something from the board of directors tomorrow. In the meantime, the Ohio governor has called in the National Guard to move all the news trucks to the state fairgrounds and to maintain crowd control here at the hospital."

"Thanks, Roberta. We're now going to switch to Jessica Laruet, our correspondent in Phoenix. Jessica, what can you tell us about the frenetic activity going on now in Arizona?"

"Daniel, it has been absolute bedlam all day here throughout the state of Arizona, and not just near the Navajo Nation. An estimated 400 thousand of what state officials are calling 'medical tourists' have flooded across its borders in what some are comparing to a modern-day Woodstock…Many are from Europe and Asia. And a lot of these people have no idea where they're going. Many of them think that the Navajo Reservation is just a village, not realizing that the Navajo Nation covers an area greater than the state of West Virginia."

I said to my two ladies, "Are we now sorry that we turned it on?"

"Jessica," said the anchor, "who are these people going to Arizona and what do they want?"

"Daniel, nearly all of the medical tourists or their loved ones have a serious illness that they are desperate to have cured. Many are burn patients like Carli. Many have some form of cancer. And they're here as a last resort because they can't find adequate treatment elsewhere. Unfortunately, their desperation has inspired a new cottage industry and I can guess that perhaps several thousand men in this state over forty years old are now falsely calling themselves medicine men and setting up healing clinics on every street corner in Phoenix and especially around the Phoenix airport. And virtually *all* of them are claiming to be the real Rising Sun."

"Jessica, are people falling for this?"

"Many are, Daniel, and they don't seem to care. As long as they can get a ten-minute healing ceremony performed by someone claiming to be a medicine man, they say it gives them hope, and they're paying upwards of five hundred to a thousand dollars for the privilege. Unfortunately, the only thing being sold at *these* clinics is false hope. This is Jessica Laruet, ABC News, Phoenix."

"We're going to turn back now to Columbus, where Roberta says she's found a witness who claims to have seen Carli Green in the hospital's prison ward. Roberta, are you there?"

"Yes, Daniel. I'm here with Tyler Shelding, who was discharged this afternoon. Although the hospital chairman has placed a gag order on employees, this man is not an employee. Mr. Shelding, why were you in the prison section of the hospital?"

"Oh, it's nothin'. I was just arrested in a bar fight last night and had my nose broke."

"So how do you know that it was actually Carli Green in the opposite cell from you?"

"Are you kiddin'? 'Cause she was the only female in the naughty ward who was screamin' her head off for two hours and cryin' on her mama's shoulder...about drove me crazy."

"So why do you think she was placed in the prison ward?"

"Are you kiddin'? Everyone knows *that*. She just tried to pull off the hoax of the century, but she got caught with her hands in the cookie jar. How can we allow criminal geniuses like Carli Green to walk amongst us law-abiding citizens? I saw her beady eyes...she's a bad apple for sure."

"Did she ever stop crying?"

"Well, eventually, the big dude, that Stanton guy, came up to us with this huge group of suits. He tells me to shut my mouth or he'll send me to bed without supper. Can you believe the nerve of that guy?"

"What did Dr. Stanton do then?"

"He tapped some guy and says 'Mr. Green, follow me into the cell.' Then he looks at the girl's back and says...and these are his exact words... 'Confirming, the patient Carli Green has no burn wounds.' And then he takes some pictures with a kind of x-ray camera and says 'Confirming, the patient Carli Green has no rods or screws in her spine,' whatever that means."

"Well, thank you for talking to us, Mr. Shelding."

"No problem."

"The rods and screws are of course the hardware installed during Carli's spinal surgery and which have mysteriously disappeared. Back to you, Daniel."

"And we'll be back after these messages."

TEN

The eighth day of our hospital ordeal had arrived and I really hoped that everything could be wrapped up by the end of the day. Laura and I were pleased to see our daughter bouncing back to what could more accurately be described as normal—at least normal considering the trauma of the past week. We had breakfast delivered. I definitely didn't want to be stepping out in public at this time. At 10:00 a.m. sharp, I again, took my seat in the conference room next to the chairman, Dr. Barrington Stanton.

"Mr. Green, I trust your family enjoyed the past two nights' accommodations better than the prison ward."

"We appreciated the transfer, sir."

"Ladies and gentlemen," said the chairman, "let's put our foot to the gas pedal today and get our work finished up. I want to be able to issue a statement later this afternoon. At this time, I'd like to turn over the meeting to our esteemed colleague from the FBI task force, Mr. Gerald Zimblist. What have you got for us, Gerald?"

"Good morning, Dr. Stanton. The FBI has completed its DNA research on this event. We collected DNA samples from the apartment, the paramedics' ambulance, the emergency ward, the ICU, and from the operating room on the day of Carli's surgery. We also drew a blood sample from her yesterday. All six of the samples were a match. Each one was identical to yesterday's blood draw. In all cases, we're talking about the same individual, Carli Green."

The chairman asked, "Did hospital records verify that Carli was a single birth? So there's no twin sister…no imposters?"

"That is correct. Now as far as the polygraphs, we administered seventy-five tests yesterday. We started with Mr. Green, Dr. Dred, and Dr. Duncan. Then we tracked down the two paramedics. Then we tested everyone who was ever in the same room with Carli Green. That included ten people in the emergency room, twelve from Dr. Duncan's operating room, five from the bathing room, two who ran the shower trolley, nine doctors, eleven nurses, five desk administrators, ten orderlies, and six custodians."

"And have you processed the results yet?"

"We have. We asked a lot of questions to all the participants, but there were two questions that we asked everyone. The first was 'Did you know Carli Green or her father Roland Green before this week?' Eight of them said 'yes,' and those were the ones who recognized her from her job in the sandwich shop across the street. The rest said 'no.' And according to the test, all of them were being truthful."

"And what was the second question?"

"We asked, 'Did you conspire to participate in a hoax with Carli Green or her father, Roland Green?' All seventy-five answered 'no' and according to the test, all of them were being truthful."

"Mr. Zimblist, we realize that was a very daunting task and we appreciate the efforts of your team. More importantly, it's a great comfort to know that all the staff members of this hospital perform their duties with the highest integrity."

"Yes, sir. We also dropped by the sandwich shop to question Carli's co-workers, and none of them noticed any special attention that Carli gave to hospital staff. They said she was friendly to everyone."

"Okay."

"And her apartment neighbors said basically, the same thing…that Carli and Marty were a nice couple, friendly…they played with their dogs in the courtyard. Nothing unusual that would indicate major problems."

"Mr. Zimblist, we are very pleased with the thoroughness of your investigation and we thank you. Moving on now…Ryan, you were working with the magicians. What have you got?"

"Sir, I posed a single question to each one. 'How would you construct a trick that would begin with the Green / Newman apartment fire and end with Carli Green having no injuries to her skin or spine?'"

"And how did they respond?"

"Well, surprisingly, all of them came up with a similar list of solutions, and I'd like to go over them one by one."

"Proceed."

"Well first, Carli switched bodies with an identical twin or a clone."

"Debunked…Ryan, when you see your first human clone, will you let me know right away, please?"

"Yes, sir. Next…Carli set the fire to their apartment."

"The fire marshal debunked that one."

"Okay, next…This was an inside job. The Greens had to have help from a number of hospital employees."

"Seventy-five lie detector tests say otherwise."

"Next…The light, the mist, and the sparklers were common parlor tricks that any magician could do."

"So what? Ryan, we're not interested in those. What we want to know is how her burns healed so quickly and why her spinal hardware is no longer in her back."

"Of course, sir. Next…Carli faked her injuries with Hollywood props and makeup."

The chairman stood up. "Dr. Dred, did you observe Carli Green's burn injuries when she first came into the ICU?"

"Yes I did, sir."

"And were those burns fake or real?"

"I believe they were real, sir."

"You believe? Our fire marshal, Mr. Barnes, also believed they were real. The nurses in the bathing room also believed they were real. And about fifty other people who saw her burns also believed they were real. I believe that claim is debunked."

"Yes, sir. Next…The spinal surgeon installed the titanium rods and screws into a cadaver spine."

Dr. Dred and Dr. Duncan immediately sprang to their feet. Dr. Dred yelled first.

"I'M THE ONE who came up with all those theories!"

Dr. Duncan followed and began shouting at the group. "NOW SEE HERE! My team worked nine hours…nine hours!…to put that poor girl back together. There's not a man or woman among you in this room with the skills to do what I did. So if you want to turn all my patients over to some voodoo hocus-pocus witch-doctor sorcerer, then go right ahead. But you'll have my resignation right now!"

The chairman stood again. "Dr. Duncan," he yelled back, "I will not tolerate hate speech in my hospital, and you are *way* over the line."

"Sorry, sir."

"Further, there will be no resignations by anyone as a result of this event. At this institution, we recognize you as one of the finest spinal surgeons in the nation, and I would like every member of the board of directors who supports Dr. Duncan to rise now."

Every member rose.

"Let the record show that this hospital does not perform fake operations… and that every member of this board of directors supports now, and will continue to support in the future, our esteemed surgeon, Dr. Logan Duncan."

"Mates." Dr. Duncan tipped his safari hat and took a seat.

"And Dr. Dred," said the chairman, "we'll all be looking forward to attending your first magic act in Vegas."

The chairman sighed. "Ryan, I'm terribly sorry I gave you this assignment. This poor idea was mine. But did you hear any other crackpot solutions from the magicians that you'd like to aggravate us with?"

"Well, sir, they said that the x-rays could have been faked or Photo-shopped."

Dr. Stanton walked over to the light board. "I took the third x-ray myself, yesterday," he said. "The first two were taken before and after the spinal surgery by Dr. Duncan. Ryan, would you like to go find someplace to hide now?"

"No, sir. I'll stay."

"Just so everyone knows," said the chairman, "I had the lab go over the first two x-rays yesterday. As difficult as it would be to fake a plastic film x-ray, it would be even *more* difficult to make titanium hardware appear to be on the inside of a human being. They went over every square inch with a microscope. Once again, it's the real deal. Anything else?"

"Just one, sir. Some of them suggested that this might be a case of mass hypnosis."

"Pardon?"

"They said that every person who came into contact with Carli could have been hypnotized into believing that Carli had these terrible injuries, but in actuality, she did not."

"Ryan, come over here to the light board, please."

"Yes, sir."

"Not that I want to pick on you, but did any of these magicians suggest how the titanium rods and screws in x-ray two could be hypnotized into not showing up on x-ray three?"

"No, sir."

"I didn't think so. Well, obviously, this exercise with the magicians was a waste of taxpayers' money, but I thank you for your efforts anyway, Ryan."

"You're welcome, sir."

"Okay, everyone, at this time, we'll break for lunch and when we return, we'll start putting together our statement for the press."

But lunch would have to wait, as there was a knock at the door. When the caller entered, the room became so quiet you could hear cliché number 270...a pin drop. It was Carli Green.

I swallowed hard and ran over to her. "Hi, dear, is something wrong?"

She just stared past me and stated bluntly to the room, "I want to take a polygraph...here and now."

"Honey, you don't have to do that. In fact, you shouldn't do it. No one is asking you to do it. Nothing good can be gained by it."

My daughter ignored me and pointed straight ahead at one person who sat on the right side of the four-table grouping. She practically yelled in my ear.

"And I want it administered by Dr. Dred! I want *her* to have to tell me if I should go to prison...again."

"Carli, this can't happen," I begged her. "You've got to just let it go. That woman's a monster." I didn't care if Dr. Dred heard me call her a monster. She stood up.

"Let her do it, Mr. Green. She's an adult, and it's her choice. The machine is still right here on the table."

Dr. Stanton was next to stand. "Miss Green, you are under no obligation to take a polygraph."

"I want to do it...now," my daughter stubbornly repeated.

Dr. Stanton looked to his left near the back of the room. "Mr. Zimblist, would the FBI allow a polygraph to be administered by someone not on your team?"

"Sir, we can set it up if you want to, but I want to make it clear that the test would in no way be official and would not be included in the report of our trip."

"I'm stopping this now," I stated.

Doctor Stanton put up a hand. "Mr. Green, I must remind you, your daughter is an adult."

"Carli, don't," I said.

"Let's do it," she overruled me.

With great frustration, I about-faced and slowly returned to my seat, thinking, "Nuclear disaster is imminent." I certainly didn't like seeing the sly smile on the face of Dr. Dred.

Gerald Zimblist, the leader of the FBI team, asked Carli to come forward and sit to the left of Dr. Dred. He brought over the polygraph machine so that Dr. Dred could see the printout results while the subject, Carli, could not.

"Miss Green, if you would please place your feet flat on the floor and spread your fingers apart on the table...I'm now going to place two pneumo-graphic breathing tubes around you, one around your chest and one around your belly. These are of course to measure your rate of breathing. Next, I'm placing a blood pressure cuff around your left arm and you'll feel a bit of a squeeze here. Now I'm going to place autonomic clips on the first and third fingers of your right hand. These will measure your heart rate, sweating, and nervous system. Do you feel comfortable enough to begin?"

"I do."

"Okay, Dr. Dred, please keep in mind that we like to limit the test ques-tions to those that have 'yes' or 'no' answers."

"Understood," replied the doctor.

"Then if both of you are ready...Dr. Dred, you may ask your first question."

"Thank you, Mr. Zimblist...and thank you, Miss Green, for coming for-ward this morning. My first question for you is, 'Have you ever engaged in espionage against the United States'?"

"No."

"Good, that was our practice question so now, let's move on...Have you ever cheated on a tax return?"

"No."

"That's a lie."

Carli started to squirm in her seat. "But it was only a hundred-dollar lot-tery ticket that I didn't declare as income."

"Have you ever shoplifted?"

"No."

"That's a lie."

"Oh my God, it was only a pair of earrings when I was in the seventh grade and I gave them back!"

"You mentioned God...Do you believe in God, Miss Green?"

The FBI leader quickly interrupted. "That's an illegal question, Dr. Dred."

"Okay, so have you ever stolen anything from a place where you worked?"

"No."

"That's a lie."

The hooked-up subject was becoming quite agitated and her breathing rate visibly increased. "Come on, it was only some bagels that were past the expiration date and they were going to throw them out anyway."

"On your way to a life of crime, aren't you, Miss Green?"

"No!"

"That's a lie too. But let's move on. Miss Green, did you set the fire at your apartment?"

"No. I absolutely did not."

"Does it bother you that millions of people think you did start it?"

"No."

"Does it bother you that millions of people think that you murdered your husband?"

"No!"

"Oh, really, Miss Green?" the doctor said, raising her voice. "Well, doesn't it bother you that millions around the globe think that you tried to pull off the hoax of the century right here at this hospital?"

"But I didn't do it!"

"Of course not. All you tried to do was fake your injuries."

"No!"

"You, your father, and that medicine man all got together in a nice little conspiracy and figured out how to make you look like a 'miracle girl' to cash in big-time on your fame. Isn't that true, Miss Green?"

From across two tables, I wondered how long it would take Dr. Dred to get *my* name into the mix…but she hadn't forgotten.

"Did your father obtain a cadaver or a cadaver spine for your surgery?"

"No! None of it is true!" yelled Carli.

"Lie after lie, Miss Green…Next question…Have you ever committed an immoral act?"

"We've heard enough," announced the FBI leader. "Dr. Dred, you will ask one more question and then we're shutting it down."

"But I'm not done. I still have more questions."

Mr. Zimblist walked around the tables till he came to Dr. Dred. "Oh, you're done all right, Doctor…and the last question is this one. Just read it right off the sheet."

"Can't I ask my own question?"

The annoyed FBI man pointed to the paper and firmly gave her a direct instruction. "Read the sheet, Doctor."

Dr. Dred did not like being ordered around, but now, she had no choice. She cleared her throat and spoke. "Miss Green, during the last eight days, did you plan or participate in a hoax at The Ohio State University Medical Center?"

"No."

"That's a lie," said the doctor.

"Dr. Dred," said Mr. Zimblist, "the needles didn't jump." Then he spoke loudly to the entire group. "Let the record show that the subject answered the last question truthfully…Let's eat."

ELEVEN

The break for lunch came none too soon. As I escorted my daughter back to the hotel room, she sniffed often, and then finally broke into tears.

"You were right, Daddy. She's a monster. It was awful. How could I do such a stupid thing?"

"You know, kiddo, one of the things I most admire about you is your stubbornness. And anyway, it all might have been worth it when you answered the last question."

She shook her head. "I'll never do that again."

"Good choice."

* * *

I ate lunch with my family this time and, afterward, returned once again to the conference room. Dr. Stanton and his group spent the next several hours reviewing the evidence, or lack thereof, in minute detail. I didn't say a word. By this time, I was totally fed up with the investigation and just wanted out…and I couldn't stand the sight of Dr. Dred.

"All right," said the chairman. "At this time, with debate concluded, I'd like to see where we stand…and I'd like a show of hands, please. How many people in this room believe that the Navajo Event was a hoax?"

My jaw dropped. It could have dropped two floors. Aside from me, every single person in the room raised their hand. Even the four emissaries from the pope had their hands up.

"And now," the chairman continued, "raise your hand if you believe that the medicine man known as Rising Sun cured Carli by performing a Navajo healing ceremony."

Of course I raised my hand…and everyone in the room stared at me as if I had two heads.

"I see that our decision is not unanimous," announced the chairman. "Mr. Green," he sighed, "could you please tell us *why* you believe the medicine man healed your daughter?"

I took a deep breath. "Because the Navajo are a gentle, quiet people who didn't come here for attention or publicity. I've been to their homes. I've broken bread with them. They just wanted to help a friend. My cousin, Dr. Green, brought them here in his plane. He could have made millions as a physician in L.A. just by staying home. Instead, he chose to live with the Navajo. Look, it may be hard to believe, but some people are just good people."

"Perhaps you're right."

"Remember when Dr. Green talked on the phone about the thirteen-year-old boy? When he showed me his picture with the amputated arms, I didn't believe for a second that Rising Sun could have reattached them and healed him. But now I do."

"And I must admit, Mr. Green, that you passed your polygraph with flying colors."

"Dr. Stanton…my family…we're just three shlabutniks."

"Pardon?"

"Commoners…nobodies…I work in accounting nine to five and then come home and do crossword puzzles. My wife is a legal secretary who cooks dinner and sews doll clothes. My daughter bakes sandwiches and then she and her husband would come home and play with the dogs. None of us has anywhere near the sophistication to create the kind of hoax you've been trying so hard to unravel here."

"Mr. Green, you make a very strong case. But could you accept our public conclusion if we still believe the Navajo Event to be a hoax? I just cannot throw my entire talented and dedicated medical team under the bus. I can't go out and publicly say something like 'wizards are better than doctors.'"

"Believe what you want," I replied. "Laura and I are just glad to have our daughter back alive and well. And further, we'd like to give great thanks to Dr. Dred and her ICU staff as well as to Dr. Duncan and his surgical team. The care they all gave Carli was nothing short of phenomenal."

Dr. Dred's eyeballs nearly popped out of their sockets. She turned her head away quickly. I knew she was crying.

Dr. Duncan came over to me and shook my hand. Then I got scared when he took out his foot long crocodile-hunting knife. He presented the handle to me.

"A souvenir, mate," he said with a grin. "I can get another. Just don't wave it around too much in the hospital…technically, no weapons are allowed."

"That's very generous of you, Dr. Duncan. I am most appreciative…and again for Carli, I thank you so much."

I followed that by moving around the room and shaking hands with every person there, even the two police officers who were in the room since the beginning.

The chairman was last. "You have a wonderful family, Mr. Green. I'm glad we had a chance to meet."

"Can we go home now, Dr. Stanton?"

"First, stop by the office and pick up Carli's discharge papers. After that, you're all welcome to join us at the press conference if you'd like."

"Thanks, Doctor," I replied, "but we're going to pass. We'll just watch it from our room while we're packing up."

The chairman placed his hand to his chin in thought. "Unfortunately, leaving might be problematic for you, Mr. Green. There are many paparazzi everywhere. If you go through the front door, you might not be able to make it to your car."

"Do you have any suggestions?"

Dr. Stanton looked to his left at the FBI team. "Mr. Zimblist?"

The lead agent walked over to me. "I've been giving this some thought, Mr. Green. One of my team members could drive your car to The Ohio State University Airport. The hospital has a helipad, so your family could just hitch a ride on a medical chopper and go over there to meet your car."

"How much would *that* cost?"

The chairman scoffed, "Mr. Green, I'm giving you instructions to ignore all hospital bills. I'll take care of everything."

"That's a very gracious offer, Doctor, one that my wife and I will gladly accept. Thank you."

"There's just one more small technicality," said Mr. Zimblist.

"Such as?" I asked.

"Well, right now, Carli is the biggest celebrity on the planet. And as we speak, some ten thousand people are filling up the streets in your neighborhood. Your house in Solon is surrounded. There are police departments from many suburbs there that are trying to keep order."

"What? Why?"

"You must understand that there's a lot of sick people out there who want the Carli Green mojo…to get as close as they can to her, to see her, better yet to touch her."

"But we're not looking for that. We're not royals from England. We just want our privacy."

"I'm afraid, Mr. Green, that the only thing we can recommend for your family now is the U.S. Marshals Service's witness protection program…get you new ID's, new house, new car, wigs, sunglasses, passports, disguises. It's a big undertaking, but I can be your liaison to them if you'd like."

I groaned, "Do we really have to do all that?"

Mr. Zimblist flipped open his laptop and entered the search term "Beatles land at JFK Airport, February 7th, 1964." It brought up a video of John, Paul, George, and Ringo disembarking from their plane on the tarmac amongst thousands of screaming people.

"Why are you showing this to me?" I asked the FBI man.

"Because this is what your life is going to look like from this day forward."

"So you're suggesting we do the witness protection program?"

"I am."

Then I sighed very deeply and shook my head as I mumbled, "Laura's just going to *love* this."

* * *

When I returned upstairs to our hotel room, Laura and Carli, as expected, were not very pleased when I explained our predicament.

"Look on the bright side," I said. "We get to ride in a helicopter."

"But where are we going to sleep tonight if we can't go home?" my wife asked me.

I shrugged. "I guess that's what moms are for."

Since it was getting close to 5:00 p.m., I clicked on the TV to watch the much anticipated press conference. I had to step a little closer to the screen because I couldn't quite believe what I was seeing. The Beatles weren't playing guitars, and the Buckeyes weren't playing football, but Ohio Stadium was completely packed with over 100 thousand attendees...for a press conference?

A podium had been set up on the fifty yard line, and I could easily recognize all the faces from the board of directors. Many of the doctors were also present in their white lab coats.

"Good afternoon, everyone," Dr. Stanton began, glancing at his notes. "Today is a day of celebration. One week ago, a young woman came to us at The Ohio State University Medical Center with horrific injuries she received as a result of an apartment fire. But today, she has earned her medical discharge. She leaves us in the peak of health. I am therefore declaring this day to be 'Carli Green Day' in Columbus, Ohio."

The members of the board and the doctors who were on the stage began to clap loudly. That spirit quickly spread throughout the huge building, and soon, 100 thousand citizens were on their feet roaring their approval and applauding along in unison.

I got goose bumps on my back, but my daughter just shook her head and said, "I don't deserve this. I didn't do anything."

The chairman continued. "All of us at this facility feel blessed to have been part of her story. But as we celebrate a life, we must also be cognizant of the bittersweet fate that accompanied this story…the loss of a wonderful and devoted husband, Marty Newman. I now ask that we all bow our heads in a moment of silence as we reflect on the different fates that await all of us in our short journeys on this earth."

The crowd fell silent for thirty seconds.

"Thank you. There are many individuals who deserve strong recognition for their contributions to what has become commonly known as the Navajo Event. First, we give thanks to Dr. Sabrina Dred…"

"Booooooooooo," Carli yelled at the TV.

"Don't do that, doll," I said. "We made up."

"How could you?"

The chairman continued. "…and her ICU staff, who worked tirelessly to get Carli through the very critical first twenty-four hours after the fire. They're challenged with life-and-death moments every day they step through our doors."

The large audience applauded again.

"I guess I forgot about that part," Carli admitted.

"Next, there's a very talented orthopedic surgeon on our staff whom we have affectionately nicknamed 'Crocodile Dundee.'"

A drone of muted laughter could be heard from the crowd.

"What Dr. Logan Duncan has done for Carli Green and for hundreds of others like her with severe spinal injuries is nothing short of miraculous."

I nodded my head and clapped along with the crowd. I liked how Dr. Stanton used the word "miraculous."

"And of course we must also thank Carli's parents, Roland and Laura Green, for their passion and devoted support that only the most loving of parents could provide."

We heard a few claps for us, too, and that was fine.

"However, the lion's share of our appreciation must go to a true American hero. Today we pay tribute to a Navajo medicine man named HA'íí'ááGO, or Rising Sun, the spiritual grandfather of his Nation, whose goal was to use his last living breath to come to Columbus, Ohio to do a good deed. And he succeeded…spectacularly."

This remark aroused great joyousness from the huge throng as I laughed and said, "Hey, that's *my* line!"

The chairman glanced again at his notes. "We don't understand how a Navajo healing ceremony works. To us, it's a mystery and perhaps it shall always remain a mystery."

He continued, "Rest assured my staff and our team from the FBI have left no stone unturned, and it is certain that more details of our investigation will be released in the coming days. What we do know for sure is that science doesn't always have the answers, and we must bear that in mind before we go around making unfounded accusations of wrongdoing. Ignorance is not evidence. Ignorance is not proof of a crime."

"You HEAR that, Dr. Dred?" Carli yelled at the TV.

"For now, the story of Carli Green may have left us all in a state of wonderment. And I for one feel honored and grateful that her story has played out in *our* facility and with our own outstanding medical staff and team members."

The crowd was getting into the groove of clapping at each pause.

"I apologize to the thousands of you who came to this press conference seeking answers to a riddle. I can tell you that it's a hard riddle and it won't be solved today. But if you believe in a supreme being, it matters not whether you call them DIYIN DiNé'E or God, or any other name. This event gives us the hope that he is out there somewhere, and listening to our prayers."

"So from all of us on the board of directors and from our entire staff, we wish all of you a great day of celebration. Thank you."

Another roar and standing ovation from the crowd brought the press conference to a fitting and pleasing finale.

"Well, that certainly wasn't what I was expecting," I said to my wife and daughter.

"Why?" asked Laura. "What *were* you expecting?"

"Well, we didn't hear anything about rods and screws and polygraphs and twins and cadavers and arson and magicians…and nothing about lights and mist and sparklers."

"BAM!" Carli's voice exploded in my face. "Dad! He didn't say the H-WORD!"

I slowly sat down on the bed. I offered her a warm smile and then I sighed, "You're right, kiddo…he never once uttered the word 'hoax.'"

TWELVE

The chore of packing up our bags continued, but after a few minutes, we were interrupted by a knock at the door. I was on guard to avoid paparazzi.

"Who's there?" I asked.

I heard a reply with a deep voice. "Officer Williams and Officer Dempsey from the conference room."

It gave me the jitters. "Are you here to arrest me?" My voice shook, and I was really afraid to hear the answer.

"Aaaaaaaaaah! Hahaha! Oh Lordy, NO!" Both officers whooped with laughter. "We actually have some good news for you."

When I opened the door, the eye contact clicked for me. The African American gentleman, Mr. Williams, was the first cop off his seat with a key when Dr. Stanton ordered me unshackled.

Now I relaxed. "Hello, come in please."

Upon entering, Officer Dempsey commented, "Congratulations on your 'day,' Carli. We were rooting for you."

She answered with a smile and a "thank you."

"So what is this good news?" I inquired.

Mr. Williams followed up. "There's a gentleman downstairs in the food court who would like to treat your family to dinner."

"Is this how it starts?" I asked him. "The media corners us and it just goes from one interview to another?"

"Oh, no, Mr. Green. This gentleman is definitely not part of the media. I talked to him a little, and he seems like a pretty nice guy. You should go."

I was still worried. "Won't there be crowds pointing at us?"

"We can take you in the service elevator and that way you can enter through the back of the food court. No one will bother you."

"Any objections?" I asked my family.

Laura and Carli looked at each other and gave me nods of approval. "Please lead the way, Officers," I directed.

The hospital seemed almost empty. I imagined that the majority were still exiting from Ohio Stadium a couple of blocks away. When we stepped off the elevator we found ourselves among the last tables in the food court. Seated in front of us at a round table was an elderly man, not surprisingly sporting both a Buckeye sweatshirt and a Buckeye baseball cap.

Officer Dempsey advised us that the gentleman wanted to sample the local cuisine and so had ordered a burger, fry, Coke combo for dinner. He asked if that would be agreeable to us and we told him, "Sure." Then he held up four fingers, which were spotted by one of the servers way up front.

Officer Williams indicated with an open hand that we were welcome to take our seats at the round table with the gentleman.

This man was definitely experienced in years as a senior citizen. There were appropriate wrinkles in appropriate places. He bore kind appearing hazel eyes and a pleasant smile. Then those eyes zeroed in on Carli.

"Hello, young one," he said in a slow but mellow voice. "I believe that the proper greeting in this part of the world is…O—H."

Carli grinned and immediately responded with the traditional reply of…"I—O."

"It is good to see that these dishes from Hamburg, Germany, have made their way to America…in addition to the hot potatoes from France…but the Coke will always be yours to boast."

"Thank you for dinner," I said. We were all anxious to burst out with the question, "Who *are* you?" But we thought it wise to let the host conduct the proceedings.

Once again, the older gentleman turned his gaze to our daughter. "Congratulations on your personal holiday, young one." He tipped his cap and added, "I very much like the sound of 'Carli Green Day.'"

The split second when he raised his baseball cap, I saw it…the white zucchetto, or beanie, that only one person on earth is permitted to wear.

I nudged Laura with my elbow and said, "Honey, I think it's the pope," then turned back to face our host. "We are most honored, Your Holiness."

Carli's eyes lit up. "Are you really a Buckeye fan?" she pried.

"I am today, young one," he answered. "You have a beautiful campus here and I was able to walk across it and view the sights without a throng."

"We're in the same boat now too," I added.

"Oh, you have a boat?"

"Uh, not exactly. Your Holiness, we were just wondering…to what do we owe this honor?"

"Mr. Green, did my emissaries tell you that we take our miracles seriously?"

"Oh, yes. They were quite emphatic in making that point. But they also raised their hands when asked if they thought that her healing was a hoax."

"…so as not to draw attention to our true beliefs."

The pope looked back at Carli. "Young one, my scientists have closely examined your case. Of the billions of people in the world, modern twenty-first-century technology has proven that you are the only one to have been touched directly by the hand of God. Your injuries were real. Your spinal surgery was real. Your x-rays *are* real. And your healed body *is* real."

The pope reached forward and gently grasped Carli's right hand, which was still holding several french fries. "Young one, you could give hope to millions who would wish just to touch the hand that was touched by God."

Carli shrugged. "But I'm just a sandwich shop girl."

"And I am just a man," the pope replied. "But the world still revolves around faith. And your presence alone will magnify faith throughout all regions of the world."

Carli drew back her hand. "What if I don't *want* to be special?" she asked, a bit of anxiety in her tone. "I was asleep during the whole Navajo Event thing that everyone keeps talking about…and I just didn't do anything."

"Young one, I am pleased to see such humility in your spirit. But trust my counsel when I tell you this…we cannot always choose our fate. Perhaps if I further explain the nature and rarity of miracles, you may come to understand that being special is a *good* thing."

The pope continued. "In your case, surviving an accident is not a miracle, just as not surviving an accident is not a miracle. To be a miracle, the event must violate the laws of nature and physics…as your third x-ray clearly shows. That x-ray, along with your current healthy state, demonstrates clear and undisputed scientific evidence that the Navajo Event, your healing, did take place."

The pontiff added, "The events that qualify as miracles should establish proof of a supernatural entity such as God or, as may be in this case, the Navajo supreme beings that I have read about, DIYIN DiNé'E. It's an event that could only be caused by a supreme being and have no other explanations."

"Uh, Your Holiness," Carli interrupted, "I have a stupid question."

"We popes have counseled for centuries that there are no inappropriate questions."

"Well, what if it's like *Star Trek* where aliens come down and use their advanced knowledge to heal us?"

"If that day ever comes, young one, those might be good deeds, but they would not be miracles."

Carli then looked at me. "Dad, do you think Rising Sun could be an alien?"

I strained my mouth's expression thinking about that. "Well, he sure didn't look like one. And he couldn't heal himself...so I would guess 'no' to answer that question."

We suddenly sensed urgency in the pope's voice. "Young one, due to these miracles, the Congregation for the Causes of Saints has urged me to rapidly elevate your status to a living saint."

I dropped my burger on my tray. Laura and Carli also dropped whatever they were holding.

Carli was clearly in shock. She shook her head back and forth rapidly. "That's CRAZY!" she blurted out. "That is just nuts! And anyway, how can you have a Jewish saint?"

The pope calmly stated, "Jesus was Jewish. So were all twelve of his disciples. Unfortunately, some of my predecessors were quite unkind to the Jewish people and to Native Americans. The inquisition in Spain and the actions of men such as Cortes and Pizarro have left dark pages in the history books from which we must emerge. An irony is that a Native American came to heal you in a city named to honor the man who began the decimation of Native Americans."

Carli's face looked empty. She moaned, "This is way...way beyond what my brain cells can process."

"Young one, even Moses asked, 'Who am I that I should bring out the children of Israel from Egypt?' When God chooses you, it's usually for a good reason."

"What would I have to do?" my daughter asked with trepidation.

The pope leaned back and smiled. "That is the easy part, young one. After your beatification, you would just sit and allow people to touch your hand. Those who are ill know that you cannot cure them, but touching the hand that was touched by God will give them hope. We all have a certain amount of faith in God, but your presence will increase that faith exponentially. Only you can do this and no one else in the world."

"Would I have to move to Vatican City?"

"Oh no, but if you could spare a thirty-day sabbatical, that would be a blessing for all. And there's a bonus for you too, if you decide to accept the title of Saint Carli of Columbus."

My daughter covered her face with her hands. The pope's last remark was both powerful and overwhelming. I suggested to my wife, "Honey, why don't you take Carli to the restroom for a minute?"

I thought, "Okay, good move…now how do I make small talk with the pope?"

He went first. "Mr. Green, do you ever watch the World Cup soccer matches?"

"Uh, not a lot…But I've heard that Pele is pretty good."

My ladies' bathroom break was mercifully brief.

Carli looked refreshed and confident when she came back to her seat.

"Your Holiness," she asserted, "please elaborate on the bonus."

"Of course. As a living saint, you are permitted to choose a patronage."

"I don't understand."

"For example, you could choose to become the patron saint of bakers… except *that* patronage is already assigned to Saint Honore."

My daughter's face brightened as she asked, "How about the patron saint of sandwiches?"

The pope shook his head. "Unfortunately, that honor has already been assigned recently to Saint Luciana of Panini…a girl younger than you, who died for her belief that a sandwich *is* a meal if it includes cheese and lettuce."

Now her brain was really crunching the data.

"Hmmmm…hmm…hmm…hmmmmmmm…Okay, okay, how about the Patron Saint of Buckeyes?"

I had to chime in, "The football team or the nut? You know, Woody Hayes already has dibs on football."

She replied, "No, I mean for all the people of Ohio."

The pope smiled. "That is a lovely thought, young one."

"Cool, and what about my beautification?"

"You already have fine inner beauty…but poor spelling. Beatification means that you are blessed and worthy of being honored. It is the final step before sainthood and canonization. But you must keep in mind that you cannot become a real saint until at least five years after your death."

"Then why are we doing all this now?"

"When we declared Mother Teresa to be a living saint, it was done because both the clergy and the masses believed that she had already qualified for her sainthood. This is similar to what we currently believe for you. So being a living saint is practice for becoming a real saint later on."

I inquired, "Okay, so Carli would be on the 'practice squad' now, but doesn't a saint have to perform three miracles?"

"It's down to two, now."

I nodded. "That's easy."

"The miracles must be *attributed* to that person. In this case, the light, the mist, and the energy particles are all considered as separate miracles."

She asked, "But wouldn't those miracles be attributed to Rising Sun, the medicine man?"

"No, young one. The miracles were directed from God to you. Rising Sun was a great man performing a good deed as the medium...or we could say as the 'Good Samaritan,' acting selflessly to help others. But God touched you. For several minutes, he held you in his arms and for that, there is indefatigable proof. A pope canonizes a person to make official, what God has already done."

"Would we have to fly to Rome now?"

"No, no. We realize that this past week has been very stressful for you and your parents. You should go home and rest. Call us when you are ready. There are just two other questions, young one. The first is, have you been a servant of God?"

Carli thought about it before answering, "I became a bat mitzvah when I was thirteen."

The pope nodded. "Ah, you are a daughter of the commandment. And have you led a life of virtue?"

"Uh...It's more like little virtues here and there. I volunteered in a soup kitchen for the poor, I was a runner for the senior center Bingo games, I rescued my dogs from the pound so they wouldn't have to be euthanized...oh, and I smile a lot."

"I see." The pope carefully weighed Carli's resume of virtues. He stated, "My definition of a 'young one' is a person who has many selfless acts yet to perform...but I will not discount your smile."

The pope reached into his pocket and gave Carli an envelope and what looked to be a business card. "The card directs you to my chief emissary, Monsignor Mateo Romano," the pontiff said. "He will handle all communications as I am, as you might expect, quite busy."

"Thank you," she replied.

"Inside the envelope is a gift from the College of Cardinals. This is the part that we don't like to talk about so much in public. A ceremony to declare a living saint can be quite an expensive occasion. And there is a large department at the Vatican whose purpose is to raise funds through the sale of remembrances."

He continued, "When you come to Rome, you should not be surprised to see your name and image on items such as coins, portraits, shot glasses, figurines, coffee mugs, dinner plates, pens, T-shirts, toothpaste, temporary tattoos, key chains, badges, watches, stuffed animals, fuzzy dice, umbrellas, coasters, bobble-heads, snow globes, ball caps, soccer balls, school stickers, bumper stickers, lipstick, soft drinks, energy drinks, Halloween masks, handbags, backpacks, backscratchers, socks, Frisbees, refrigerator magnets, pillowcases, calendars, socks, helium balloons, cereal boxes, bibs, bubble gum, bubble bath, piggy banks, Chia Pets, pajamas, beach towels, sun visors, stationery, stationary bikes, phone cases, color by number kits, mail boxes, headphones, Happy Meal prizes, postcards, trading cards, playing cards, Christmas cards, and even candy bars."

My daughter looked across the table at me with almost a blank stare. "Dad, I'm not going to be able to handle all this."

"Well, we could always use a few more refrigerator magnets, but why don't you see what's in the envelope?"

Carli tore open the flap and immediately put her right hand to the side of her head. Her mouth remained wide open. When the check was passed to my wife, she did the same...and when it was passed to me, I did the same too.

"Your Holiness," Carli said, "three million dollars is more than generous. We don't know what to say except thank you very much."

The pope leaned back and smiled. "A million dollars per miracle seemed like a nice round number."

THIRTEEN—POV Carli

The next morning we rose early to hop on our ride in the medevac to The Ohio State University Airport. It felt a bit scary as none of us had ever ridden in a helicopter before. But it was certainly the best means of escape as the crowd in front of the hospital had not dissipated. "Carli-mania" was still in full force.

True to their word, the FBI had our car waiting for us. "I'd better drive safely," my father said, "since we have the Patron Saint of Buckeyes riding with us."

"It's not funny, Dad," I complained. "I have to keep my head down so nobody recognizes me. And I want to start exercising a little more independence. I totally appreciate what you and Mom have done for me this week, but I'm not spaced out on meds anymore, and I'm not a child."

"I know, doll," he replied. "No one is standing in your way."

* * *

The choice of visiting grandmas was an easy one. Mom's side had a different last name than we did. She warned us that the police had cordoned off our house in Solon, but that there still were at least ten thousand folks milling around.

Knowing that we couldn't go anywhere in public gave us the incentive to hurry into the U.S. Marshals Service's witness protection program. Mr. Zimblist had followed us up Interstate-71 and took a personal interest in our case.

"Black wigs for all," he recommended, "and some thick-framed glasses. Use the sunglass clips when you're outdoors. Carli, you should darken your eyebrows to black, too, so they match."

"What about driver's licenses?" I asked.

Mr. Zimblist advised, "Let me photocopy what you have for those and your passports. I'll take care of them as soon as possible, but first, you need to pick out new names. Everything in your lives from now on should be as boring and non-descript as possible.

"Boring and non-descript is in our DNA," my dad said.

"Here, I'll give you a start. Your last name is now Johnson."

"Okay," I replied, "but for first names, can we just change a letter so we can still call each other basically the same thing? Can we make it sound Latin, like Rolando, Lauretta, and Carlita?"

"No way, Carli, that's too close. If you think you're still going to be able to be called Carli for short, that's not going to work at all. People will pick up on that because you're so famous."

"CASSIE!" I exclaimed. "I like that name. You know…sassy Cassie… Cassie Johnson."

"Very good," said Mr. Zimblist. "Roland, you can't go with any 'Rol's.' Why don't you try Robert Johnson? Your wife can still call you Ro if she wants."

"Then what would we do for me?" asked Mom.

"You could maybe go with a different spelling…like Lorena. He could still call you Lor, as you're not as famous as the other two. The important thing is that you don't get the names mixed up in public. You shouldn't have to think about what to call a family member."

* * *

We gradually got used to a new modest home within a gated community in Beachwood, Ohio. When we needed things from our abandoned house in Solon, occasionally the police would escort us through the back door at 3:00 a.m. Mom and Dad missed this home very much but losing it was the price we had to pay for fame we didn't want. I hadn't lived there since high school, so it didn't really bother me. Moving back in with my parents seemed the logical thing to do for now.

Mr. Zimblist took care of all the "switcheroos" between houses and cars, insisting that we drive white cars only because that was the most popular color and he didn't want us to stand out. We also tested our black wigs and disguises, shopping at Walmart but refusing to pick up any "Navajo Event" T-shirts. Walking through the mall was peaceful too and we didn't have a problem. It was kind of nice.

For a few days, we watched the 6:30 p.m. news on TV, but that got old really fast. We got tired hearing about "us" all the time, and most of the rumors about the Navajo Event were a bunch of phony baloney anyway. It reminded me too much of Dr. Dred. Every night we had to hear about how the Green family perpetrated the hoax of the century. So we took a vote and literally yanked the plug on every TV in the house.

After a couple of weeks of vegging out, I knew it was now time to take care of my responsibilities. All of us were a bit nervous about driving back to Columbus, but that, along with a flight to the Navajo Nation, were on our agenda. I picked up my cell phone.

"Bill? Hey, this is your cousin Carli. Would this weekend be an okay time for us to fly in and pay our respects?"

"It would be a perfect time, Carli. The town of Kayenta is scheduled to hold a pow-wow this weekend, but if they know you're coming in, then I'm sure they'll want to move it to Chinle. That's the town with the big clinic where I work."

"But why would they move it just for me?"

"Ha! Are you serious, Carli? Don't you watch the news?"

"It's something that we're trying very hard to avoid."

"You're a heroine. That's all people around here talk about…the recipient of the final good deed of our revered medicine man, Rising Sun."

"But I'm Caucasian."

"You're considered a friend because you're part of my family. Our economy is booming because of the 'Event.' We have about three hundred tribal elders who are medicine men to serve the endless crush of medical tourists."

My dad interrupted, "Are these tourists desperate, or are some even gullible?"

"You don't understand, Roland. They don't care if their loved one is healed or not. And they don't care if it's not performed by Rising Sun. Once they figured out that the medicine men in Phoenix were fakes, they started driving north. For one thousand dollars, they expect a genuine Navajo healing ceremony performed by a real Navajo medicine man right here in the Navajo Nation. Roland, what they're buying is hope. That's all they want. "

I asked, "Are these elders all real medicine men?"

"Oh yes. There used to be over a thousand. But many have died off without training apprentices. I think that's going to change, though. The DiNé College, just east of Chinle, has started a new Healing Practitioner Program that's attracting young students to become medicine men and women. It covers the basics, but like Caring Arms, they would still need to apprentice with an elder."

Bill continued, "But not too many tourists have managed to find their way to Chinle. We're definitely out in the middle of nowhere. So if you're planning on coming out, you should probably fly into Santa Fe, New Mexico and I can meet you there with my plane. It's only an hour flight back."

"So Saturday morning works?"

"You bet, Carli, see you then."

"Oh wait! Bill, when you see us we may be in our disguises, you know, part of witness protection."

"Ha! You guys kill me. Okay, so when I come to the airport, I'll look for three people who look like Groucho Marx."

* * *

Our early start on Friday morning got us to the Pickerington Cemetery at 10:00 a.m. By pre-arrangement, the Newman family was there to meet us. We hugged. It was low key, nothing formal.

I told my Father-in-law, Hayward, that I still struggled with survivors' guilt.

He grabbed my shoulder and said, "Forget about it, Carli. We're just the little humans here. We don't decide who lives and who doesn't. God does. And we were as thrilled as anybody when we heard about your miracles. We're really happy to see you guys here."

"Thanks," I said, wiping a tear from my eye.

From the car path, we walked about fifty feet to Marty's gravesite whereupon several objects piqued our curiosity. There were three tiny urns that stood along the stone border and a zip-lock bag underneath them with a paper noting in marking pen, "TO CARLI GREEN."

Mr. Newman advised us, "These have been here for over a week now and we've made sure nothing was disturbed until you arrived."

In an instant, I knew exactly what they were…the cremated remains of our two beagles, Snoopy and Charlie Brown, along with a smaller urn for Tommy the cat.

I was overcome with sorrow and I handed the note to my dad while Mom fished out some tissues from her purse.

Dad began reading the note aloud. "Dear Carli…We love you and we hope that you are doing well. Many of us here at the apartment prayed for you and Marty on that awful night. We thought there was nothing else we could do. But that wasn't so. Since most of us owned pets, we decided to take up a collection to honor your companion animals in a dignified and respectful commemoration."

Dad continued, "You may want to keep their remains as is, or you may want to spread their ashes at a place that meant something special to you and your pets. The choice is yours. But before you leave for home, PLEASE! PLEASE! PLEASE! Stop by the shrine in front of your apartment. That is also a permanent gift to you…Loving you…Missing you…Thinking about you all the time…From all your friends back at the apartment."

He finally exhaled. "Wow, that was really nice."

75

As I folded up the letter, I noticed a boy about twelve years old in a motorized wheelchair, rolling across the ground toward us. He was holding a box on his lap.

"That's our neighbor boy, Jimmy," Hayward told me.

"Hello, everyone," the boy said cheerfully. "I'm going to release two white doves for Marty. But don't worry. They're actually homing pigeons and they'll find their way back."

"What do the doves mean?" I asked the boy.

"Well, it's like two separate spirits," Jimmy replied. "The first one symbolizes the departing of the dead person's spirit, and the second one symbolizes the spirit of his guardian angel."

"Thanks, Jimmy. My family also has a tradition. We're going to leave three small stones on the gravesite so that Marty's spirit will know he's had visitors."

The boy opened the top of the box and we watched as the birds flew off gracefully to their destinations. By now, I needed some alone time with my husband, and my parents gently directed the group to return to the car path as I sat down in front of the gravesite.

I guess I'm not a very good mourner. I missed the funeral and now I'm sitting here trying to hide the fact from everyone that I'm not sad, but really angry...at both of us. We slept upstairs and yet never talked about a fire escape plan, never bought a chain escape ladder, never checked the lamp cord...and angry at myself because I let fear affect rational thinking. I knew that oxygen feeds a fire, so why did I open the window? I'm sorry, Marty. I wish that Rising Sun had come a few days earlier with enough strength to heal us both.

While I sat, I could hear in the background my dad trying to describe to Hayward in as much detail as possible, the chaotic week we spent in the hospital along with the unexpected visit from His Holiness. His revelations evoked the following responses from Marty's father.

"Are you kidding?!"

"Are you kidding?!"

"Are you kidding?!"

"Are you kidding?!"

"Really, Hayward," Dad said, "I'm not kidding."

When I was ready, I stood and returned to the car path where my in-laws tried to comfort me.

I reached into my jacket pocket. "There's something I'd like to give you," I told them, and handed them an envelope. "When I met the pope, he gifted me for three miracles…and I'd like to give one of those miracles to Marty."

The two parents look puzzled. "I don't understand, Carli," said Hally.

"Should we open it now?" asked Hayward.

"Yes, please."

Hayward tore open the envelope. Dad had said that the most memorable time he saw eyeballs popping out of their orbital sockets was when Dr. Dred accused Dr. Duncan of operating on a cadaver.

"ARE YOU KIDDING?" their voices exploded in unison.

Mr. Newman's hands trembled as he viewed all the zeroes on the check. "A million dollars? Seriously? But why, Carli? What are we supposed to do with it?"

"Do good deeds," I replied. "That was Rising Sun's mission when he came to Columbus to help me."

Both parents shook their heads. "We don't know what to say," said Hally.

"The words 'thank you' seem so inadequate," added Hayward.

I dismissed their concerns. "Those words work for me…and might I add 'you're welcome.'"

"Carli, can I hold your hand now?" the boy asked as he shifted his motorized chair into top speed.

"Why, Jimmy?"

The boy laughed as he shouted, "'Cause everybody wants the Carli Green mojo!"

He wheeled a fast circle (a doughnut) around me and explained. "It's just like the cooties in school. Once I touch you, I get your mojo. And wait till the other kids find out that I met you in person…the most famous girl in the world! O-M-G!" the boy squealed. "Then they'll touch my hand and every kid in school will have your mojo!"

Hally asked sheepishly, "Am I the only one who doesn't know what mojo is?"

Jimmy answered, "It's her magic superpowers. I know she can't cure me, but no one's got more mojo than Carli."

"Okay, Jimmy, you can let go now," I suggested.

My right hand played tug-of-war with the boy for at least a full minute. "Uh, Dad, are there thousands who want to do this?"

"Millions," he replied.

I cheated by raising my hand higher than the seated boy could reach. The front two wheels of his motorized chair rose up a few inches, and he eventually lost his grip.

"Thanks, Carli!" the boy shouted as he sped off toward his parents' car.

Each of the three of us picked up an urn. The Newmans thanked us again for the "miracle" donation and wished us well on our travels to Arizona. "And stay off the Internet," Hayward advised me.

"Do I need to ask why?"

"Too many conspiracy theories. It irks me when these nut-jobs still say that you killed Marty. We'll never catch a break, Carli. You were right to go into witness protection. So don't tell us if you're now Mr. and Mrs. Smith. Send us a snail mail if you have to."

"Will do," I responded.

"And Hally and I can say we met the Patron Saint of Buckeyes. Won't *that* be a hoot when you guys visit Rome? Do you have the pope's number on speed dial?"

"Nope, just his emissary…Hey, folks, we've got to run."

"Then as they said to John Glenn, God speed."

* * *

I directed my dad to drive north to Wolfe Park near the center of Columbus, where we parked and then walked a few hundred feet to the pedestrian bridge over Alum Creek.

"This park is where we had the most fun walking our dogs," I explained. "We would bring picnic lunches here that included doggie lunches too."

With the opening of each urn, I talked about that pet's personality and what made him special. Then I spread his ashes into the Alum Creek. Although Tommy the cat was never brought here, I wanted the kitty to join his playmates in the commemoration.

"Next is the apartment," my dad said.

"I don't want to go," I snapped at him. "Too recent…too painful."

"Carli, there were three capitalized 'Pleases' in the note. Your friends at the apartment must have done something really nice and they desperately want you to see it."

I buried my face into the fabric of the back seat. "I can't go there. Can't you see that?"

Mom murmured something into Dad's ear…a compromise?

"Okay, Carli, let's do this…We'll drive by the apartment and you don't have to get out of the car. In fact, you can keep your eyes closed the whole time. If there's something there we think you might want to see, we'll tell you."

"Fine," I grumbled.

With that, we set out on a fifteen-minute drive back to the east side of Columbus. I was feeling very anxious, turning onto the street of my former townhouse apartment. But I decided to peek. From a quarter mile away, I could already tell that something was different. A homemade shrine stretched the length of the complex. Thousands of colorful items lined the sidewalk… banners, flowers, cards, teddy bears, and lots of Ohio State paraphernalia. From it all, though, one item stood out. I thought, "What am I looking at? What in the world is that?"

The closer we got, the wider my eyes peeled back. It was some kind of statue. It looked like a huge bird, reflecting the sun in my eyes. But I couldn't stop staring at it. Was the location a mistake? This magnificent metallic bird spread its wings in a wide elongated U-formation that must have exceeded a span of ten feet. There was a tangle of shiny metal that formed the base while the bird itself rose quite majestically to the height of the second-story window…the one that we had used to make our escape from the fire.

"Uh, Carli…you might want to open your eyes now."

They were already open. "Wow…What is it?" I whispered.

Dad took a deep breath. "I believe what we're looking at is 'Phoenix Rising From the Ashes.' It's a colossal bird from Greek mythology who dies in a fire, but then miraculously comes back to life. It was said to cry tears that could heal anything."

"I'm going to get through this," I said, coaching myself up. "They put the statue on the spot where I landed."

A group of about a dozen people were milling around near the beautiful icon. A few of them appeared to be kneeling down, putting on some finishing touches.

"I know them!" I burst out. "Let's get out of the car."

This was the first time that I had run since before the accident. I dove into a warm embrace with my good friend, Libby, who I had learned called my dad on the awful morning. Our happy chatter was going a mile a minute as the rest of the group quickly surrounded us.

"So you saw our letter?" Libby asked.

"I did, and it's a good thing you told me to come here."

"You wouldn't believe this place since you left, girl. Every night, everyone in the complex comes to the courtyard and we sit and talk about you and Marty for hours."

"Seems like the whole world has been doing that."

When we broke our embrace, I pointed at my friend's attire. "What kind of sweatshirt is that?"

Libby pointed at the images noting, "Everyone wants Navajo Event gear now…'cause it played out right here on our OSU campus and at our apartment. Here's your light, your mist, and your energy particles. Do you want me to get you one?"

"Hmm…since I'm trying to keep my identity a secret, that would be a 'no.' But tell me about this Phoenix bird. What's up with that?"

"Well, it's a bird from Greek mythology—"

"Yeah, yeah, I got that part. What I want to know is who made it. Who built it?"

A young man stepped forward. "Hi, Carli, I'm Doug. I'm a grad student at Ohio State's Department of Art. All of us knew you were a Buckeye alum and we wanted to make a contribution to your story. But I guess we'd have to say that your story has become more of a legend now."

"What's it made from?"

"Mostly stainless steel. We had over a hundred students working on it… each had their own piece and had to follow the plan we drew up on the CAD."

"CAD?"

"Computer-aided design…we created a 3-D model first. But here, let me show you the back."

Doug guided me to the rear of the statue and pointed. "The spine of the Phoenix is constructed of a six-foot length of titanium rods and screws. This is you, Carli, rising from the ashes…Aw, don't cry."

"I'm good, I'm really good," I insisted. "Tell everyone there that I'm thankful to have such great friends."

Libby suggested, "Why don't you take home some of these teddy bears or cards. The landlord says he's going to leave your apartment exactly as is. No one will ever live there again…part of the shrine. So if you want, you could still go in and retrieve some of your personal stuff."

"No, I'm going to pass on that. The items my dad brought out smell like smoke and I don't want any more reminders. But the Phoenix is really great, thank you…and see if you can maybe give the teddy bears to a preschool or someplace like a children's hospital."

I departed after laying on a good bear hug to every member of the group…and no one asked for my mojo.

FOURTEEN

The previous day settled well in our systems and we were able to get a good night's sleep at a hotel near the Port Columbus Airport. An early flight to Santa Fe, New Mexico offered much anticipation for our Saturday trek to the Navajo Nation.

Wigs and sunglasses were mandatory on the flight. Dad related what he thought would have happened to the Beatles had they been trapped on a crowded commercial flight for four hours. So here we were, the Johnson family, off for our first sojourn with fake ID's in hand.

We deplaned via rolling staircase right onto the tarmac. Since Bill was a pilot, he had privileges to meet us there, and he was right on time.

"HEY, GROUCHO!" he yelled to us from one hundred feet away. And when he got closer, the ribbing continued. "Those are some of the worst disguises I have ever seen. You people are positively ugly! I'm ashamed to call you family."

"Well, you're stuck with us," I said to our cousin. "And you're pretty famous, yourself."

"True, but no one outside the Nation can find Chinle on a map, so I'm fairly well insulated from becoming a rock star like you guys."

My dad approached his cousin. "I have one question, Bill…and I'm really serious."

"Okay."

"Is your plane safe?"

"Oh, yes…I carry enough parachutes for everyone. Come on, let's get going. I'll give you a flying lesson along the way."

"Why would I need one?"

"*Someone's* got to fly the plane while I take my nap."

"But you said it was only an hour flight."

"Roland, you once asked me if the tourists who come to Arizona are gullible. Right now, I'd have to say yes…very."

Bill led us about three hundred feet down the tarmac to where he had parked his Piper Saratoga six-seater. Dad seemed downright scared squeezing me and Mom inside in the middle row, but he knew he had no choice. Bill pointed him to the front. Dad was riding shotgun.

"The most fun parts are the takeoffs and landings," he added.

I think what he really meant was the scariest. Santa Fe wasn't very busy, so he was able to taxi directly to the runway and get clearance from the tower.

"NC3PO you are cleared for takeoff."

I tapped Dad's cousin's shoulder from behind. "Seriously? C3PO? You named your plane after a *Star Wars* character?"

He nodded. "No one else was using it. Is everyone buckled in?"

Dad asked, "Where did you say you kept the parachutes?"

"We're throttle up, Roland."

Our engine roared to life and we were barreling down the runway. Dad's running commentary was becoming annoying.

"This doesn't feel right. It's too fast. We're running out of runway. Why aren't you yelling MAYDAY? We're off the ground. We're too high to jump out! We're trapped in a flying coffin! How can you remain calm when we could all fall out of the sky like a rock and be dead? Could this possibly get any worse?"

"Are you ready to try flying the plane, Roland?"

"Really?" Dad squeaked.

"Just baby steps first. We'll make a slight left turn. I'll work the ailerons and rudder; you just steer…like your car, only pull back slightly as we turn so we don't lose altitude."

* * *

Dad was starting to get the hang of it. Bill never took his threatened nap, so we had time to review some of the details of our upcoming visit. I poked my head in between the two front seats.

"How big of a town is Chinle?" I asked.

"We have about 4,500 souls, out of 165,000 in the Nation. Doesn't sound like much, but compared to most of the ninety Navajo towns, we are New York City…modern high school, modern clinic where I work…We've even got a Burger King now."

"Civilization has arrived."

"Civilization maybe, but the Double Bacon Cheese Whopper has yet to make inroads into Navajo cuisine. There's also a Best Western down the street, and you'll be staying there tonight. Most of the tourists here are visiting the Canyon de Chelly National Monument nearby. But do yourselves a favor and stash the Groucho Marx costumes. You won't be needing them here."

"Do they speak English or Navajo in Chinle?"

83

"At home, it's mostly Navajo. In public, it's more English. But Mama Bear will help you through all the cultural activities. She's a very doting mother, especially today when her son becomes anointed as the Nation's new primo medicine man."

Dad looked up. "Wait, you mean the boy with the drum?"

"Not a boy anymore, Roland. When Rising Sun healed his arms after his accident, he changed his name from Little Bear to AGAAN 'AA HASTí, Caring Arms…and has been dedicating his life to helping others at the clinic. He's been at my side for the last four years now soaking up knowledge. And big plans await…DiNé college and then medical school."

"That's really impressive," I said.

"Ah, but the *most* impressive step happens today when he graduates from being Rising Sun's protégé to become the big guy himself…and he can't do it without you."

Bill explained, "Carli, throughout the Navajo Nation, it is an absolute given that Rising Sun's spirit flows through your blood. He gave his last gifts and his last breath of life to you before he passed."

"So what should I do?"

"You'll transfer Rising Sun's pendant and place it over the neck of the new medicine man."

Dad looked at his cousin. "Bill, are you saying that it was the pendant that gave Rising Sun his healing powers?"

"That's the legend. That pendant has been passed down through many generations of medicine men. Its black stone is called the 'healing stone.' No one knows when it started or where it came from."

I inquired, "Do you believe it?"

"I started believing in it when I saw the boy healed. We both know that what happened to him and what happened to you are physically inconceivable. But I think it's bad karma to question good fortune…so we should just leave it alone."

"How many people are expected to come to the pow-wow?"

"Well, originally it would have been about two thousand, but when word got out that you were coming…hmm…you can bump that up now to about twenty thousand."

"Yikes!…Why?"

"We're not *that* backward, Carli. Nearly everyone's got a TV, and every night, the cable news talks about you and the Navajo Nation…or more

<u>Legend</u>

50 arrowheads represent the tribe's protection in the 50 states.

The three lines of the inner circle are a rainbow which represents the sovereignty of the Navajo Nation.

The open top is the east, the place of the rising sun.

Traditional livestock in center: horse, cow, sheep.

Two corn plants represent the sustainer of Navajo life.

Yellow pollen on the corn is used in many sacred ceremonies.

<u>4 sacred mountains:</u>

1) top, east, Blanca Peak, white represents White Shell Woman.

2) right, south, Mt. Taylor, blue color, Turquoise Woman.

3) bottom, west, San Francisco peaks, yellow, Abalone Woman.

4) left, north, Hesperus Mountain, black, Jet Woman.

specifically, the Navajo Event. It has to be the most exciting thing that's ever happened here. This is a MAJOR deal."

"Where can you put so many people?"

"The high school football stadium and the field itself, speaking of which…folks, I'm going to bank the plane now so you can look out your right side windows…here we come."

We could see the football grounds getting closer, and there were definitely a lot of people gathered already. Many were lined up to create geometric figures on the grass. As the plane swung around, we could now make out that the people had formed the letters of a greeting.

"HóSHDéíí CARLI" was spelled out between the twenty-yard line markers.

We all said "Wow" in unison, and Mom took a picture of it with her phone.

"You folks need a translation?" asked Bill.

I answered, "I'm hoping it says 'Welcome Carli.' If it doesn't, we should turn the plane around."

"Good job. You already speak Navajo. We're turning the plane around anyway. Make sure you're all buckled in for our landing."

"Doesn't this airport have a control tower," I asked.

"Would be a waste…If we get one plane, it's considered a busy day."

We felt a little more comfortable on the landing, and Bill taxied to the lot, which could park up to six airplanes. There were no hangars.

"Not exactly O'Hare," he admitted, "but it meets our needs."

Bill invited our family to pile into his SUV for the short ride back to the football field. All of us were getting goose bumps as we neared the open end of the stadium. Already, people were pointing at our vehicle and yelling my name.

"Bill, are you allowed to drive right onto the field like this?"

"Today I am. Hey, Carli, I'm opening the sun roof. Stand in the middle and wave at the crowd."

And so I did…to a thunderous ovation…like nothing I had ever heard before. If I wanted to hide from fame, this would not be the place. Today in the Navajo Nation, Carli Green was a VIP.

A trio of faces met us at the fifty-yard line. Mama Bear remembered how to greet us with her bear hug…Squeeze them until they can no longer breathe. Her blue outfit looked like it might have been designed by a geometry class. Her daughter, Bluebird, barely touched us in comparison.

But it was the proud young man who forged the greatest impression. Caring Arms appeared nothing like the little boy with the drum whom I had seen here on vacation years ago. He was now regal-looking…and without a doubt much taller…and stronger. I respectfully walked up to him and said, "You look like—"

"Like Rising Sun?" he said, finishing my words with a smile. "It was his wish to be buried with nothing…and he chose me as his successor, insisting that I wear all of the jewels, especially on the day of my anointment as the new medicine man."

"You are in full regalia," I complimented him.

He was quick to remind me, "Not yet, Carli. I am nothing without the pendant…and only the spirit of my predecessor can transfer the power of the pendant."

I nodded. "So I've been told…and I hope I've brought a little spirit for you today."

"Yes, you have," Caring Arms agreed. "Although the vessel of this spirit has blonde hair and blue eyes. Those are unusual features for a Navajo girl."

"They're kind of unusual for a Jewish girl too."

Caring Arms took a deep bow. "Carli, I would be extremely honored if you would be willing to serve as my anointer at today's ceremony. As you have been told, Rising Sun's spirit runs through your blood only…and no one else's. That fact allows you to be symbolically adopted into the Navajo Nation, just for today, and we must do so first, before you are permitted to place the pendant around my neck."

There was caution in my response. "Would I be a real Navajo?"

"No, it would just be part of today's pow-wow pageantry. Mama Bear will adopt you and guide you through the day's activities. I think you will find them enjoyable."

The large woman put her arm around my shoulder. "Look around you at these thousands of people. There will never come another day when so many pour out their love to you. You are their heroine."

I looked up at her and smiled. "Let's do it, Mama Bear."

"Splendid, Shi-YáZHí" (my little one). "Our own people are called DiNé and you must first choose a name that you will call yourself when you are among the DiNé."

It took me about a billionth of a second to make a decision. "I wish to be called 'Phoenix Rising,'"

"Excellent choice, Shi-YáZHí. You will be a great bird. Now come with me to the changing tent used for the women who are participating in the pow-wow dances. We'll find you something appropriate to wear. At the big pow-wows, they always bring some extra outfits."

As I looked around the field, the view of hundreds of dancers was an absolute kaleidoscope of color.

"All the flashy hues come out for the pow-wow," Caring Arms explained. "We have some great competitions here."

I was awed by the variety of the designs and said, "I feel like I'm in an art museum that has come alive."

"At the pow-wows, dancers are allowed to improvise and use designs from other tribes if they want to. That's why you see some with feathers."

In the changing tent, there was no shortage of volunteers offering us terrific outfits for me to wear, but one really fit my new name.

"Oh, turn your head," Caring Arms said to my parents. "Here comes Phoenix Rising."

Neither of them recognized me. Mama Bear had picked out a stunner of an outfit and Mom started snapping pictures from all angles. Our small group clapped their approval for this wardrobe that resembled a great red bird.

Mama Bear pointed out the details. "She starts with a red cotton dress with geometric designs, ten-inch hanging flower earrings with a matching double vest, orange and blue moccasin boots, blue rope belt, patterned headband with a double white plume—"

Bill posed a question. "Can the great bird spread her wings?"

Mama Bear gave me a nudge. "Show them, Phoenix."

Now they saw what was meant by "full regalia." My outstretched arms became a red wingspan of pomp and swagger...with much color in the shapes of red diamonds. The long, multi-colored fringe at the bottom of the shawl gave me the appearance of a great bird in flight.

I was beaming. I twirled around several times and then anxiously asked Mama Bear, "Can I keep it?"

"Ordinarily no, but perhaps an exception can be made for the spirit of Rising Sun. Come, SHi-YáZHí, it is time for you to create a sacred sand painting. This is called 'iiKááH' and is part of all Holyway ceremonies. A sand painting is a place where gods come and go. The healing spirits emerge from the painting and go into the patient or the healer...in this case, Caring

Arms. Traditionally, these are dry and take several days to make, but recently, it has become more popular with families when our parents and children discovered white glue."

"Where was that?" I asked.

"Walmart."

The sand painting tent did have a lot of grownups with kids in tow, creating their works of art. I was first instructed to draw a half sun placed on the horizon, which made sense considering my embodied spirit.

Mama Bear followed up. "Okay, everything else should be drawn as straight lines. You know what to do, Phoenix. Above that, the light can be arrows, water droplets can be triangles, and the energy particles can be little squares. And maybe off to the side you can draw your Phoenix Rising."

This was fun. I squeezed the white school glue on the half sun and then sprinkled yellow sand on top, waited a few seconds, and then picked up the paper and shook off all the extra sand. That was easy—a perfect yellow semi-circle. Then I just repeated the procedure with all the other objects on the painting.

I thought, "Voila...It was done."

"Beautiful job, Phoenix!" Mama Bear lavished her praise. "You can bring your painting to the ceremony and definitely take it home with you. So are you ready for the main event?"

"Already?" I asked. "Like right now?"

"Soon, SHi-YáZHí. The first group of dancers will be completing their competition in about thirty minutes."

* * *

Our party was directed to the fifty yard line by Blue Wolf, the highest ranking member (or speaker) of the Navajo Nation Council, where he was joined by all twenty-four of their delegates.

He used a wireless microphone to commence the proceedings.

"Welcome all, to the Navajo Nation ATS' OS Bee ALZHiSHí, our pow-wow in Chinle, Arizona, where we have arrived at today's main order of business, the anointing of a successor to the grandfather of our nation, the medicine man known as HA'íí'ááGO...Rising Sun."

The crowd applauded.

"The anointment is scheduled to be performed by Phoenix Rising, whom most of you are more familiar with as Carli Green...after she is symbolically adopted into the Navajo Nation."

I stood, confident and smiling in my flaming red-bird attire.

The Speaker placed one hand on my shoulder and raised the other, asking the crowd for silence. "The council has closely studied your relationship with HA'íí'ááGO, and by a unanimous decision, the council has ruled that since the man did not recover, then the spirit of Rising Sun must have departed during the time of your healing ceremony and he placed it into your body for safekeeping. Therefore, the symbolic adoption may proceed. Everyone will now sing the HóZHóJi, the Blessingway song to insure good luck and prosperity."

Blue Wolf next turned to Mama Bear and tapped two fingers on his turquoise wristwatch. "Dancers are waiting to compete."

She acknowledged his "hurry up" cue and borrowed the mic from his hand.

As the chanting and drumming picked up, Mama Bear presented me with a written card. I was a bit nervous.

"Can you read this SHi-YáZHí ? Just do your best to pronounce the words."

Mama Bear held the mic up to my lips. I was a little confused looking at the letters, but was willing to give it a go.

"AYóó áNííNíSH'Ní SHiMá…I love you, Mother."

"Good job, Phoenix…Now let me read my words to you."…Mama Bear placed her large hands on both sides of my face. "AYóó áNííNíSH'Ní ACH'é'é…I love you, Daughter."

Blue Wolf waved a hand in the air, saying, "The symbolic adoption is complete. For the duration of the pow-wow, Phoenix Rising is now DiNé, a member of the Navajo Nation,"…while the crowd roared its approval.

He added, "You may retain the clothing of your adoption. The anointing of a new medicine man will now proceed."

"Oh wow! Thanks!" I said, knowing that I could now bring the red-bird outfit back home as a precious souvenir. Mama Bear gave me a card for "thank you very much," which I tried my best to read. "T'áá ííYiSíí AHéHEé."

Blue Wolf replied with, "AOó" (you're welcome). "Your duty now, Phoenix Rising, is to transform Caring Arms from one of the Earth People to one of the Holy People…the DiYiN DiNé'E."

Mama Bear gave me what looked like a small watering can with a spout. "We will use corn oil for the anointment, daughter. Caring Arms will lean back and then you want to pour a little on his forehead."

"Won't it drip all over?"

"Just use a little bit."

Caring Arms and I did as we were instructed.

And now, a hush fell across the massive audience. I wondered how, without prompting, twenty thousand persons could become simultaneously silent, and frozen in place...such was the reverence for a single article in a leather satchel being brought to the center of the field by Caring Arm's sister, DóLii YáZHí (Little Bluebird). I could hear each step of her moccasins on the soft ground.

There was unseen anticipation building as Mama Bear slowly removed the article from the satchel. In the bright sunshine, the pendant revealed its bedazzling array of outer jewels, and she carefully passed it to me.

Caring Arms bowed his head. All were still quiet. As I delicately draped the pendant around his neck, I came face-to-face for the first time with the mysterious black rectangular healing stone that occupied the center and fell to the level of the young man's navel.

Mama Bear gave me another card. "Daughter, you will now recite the blessing."

"Okay, here we go...BEE i £ HóZHóó BEE HiNiSHNá." (Well may this glowing heart rejoice.)

Caring Arms was next. "BEE i £ HóZHóó BEE HiNiSHNá."

Blue Wolf assumed the mic again and told the enthusiastic crowd, "We now have a new medicine man...and in accordance with long-established tradition of our ancestors, when a female anoints a new medicine man, she has automatically agreed to become his wife."

My head snapped up as adrenaline bolted down my spine. "Wait, WHAT?!"

The crowd erupted in joyous applause.

I screamed out, "MAMA BEAR, HELP!"

The new medicine man casually walked up to me and said, "Blue Wolf is just messing with you, Phoenix. A brother and sister couldn't marry anyway. Please don't be too angry at him."

My parents asked me if I was okay and I answered, "Just relieved...very relieved."

Dad babbled, "Carli...Cassie...Phoenix...So after this prank, do you still want to make your presentation?"

"Absolutely," I asserted. "Mama Bear, can I borrow the mic, please?"

I took out a note card and spoke loudly to the huge throng of spectators. "Yá' áT' ééH…Hello, everyone. Becoming a member of the DiNé, the Navajo Nation for today's pow-wow, is the greatest honor of my life. And I will try to say again T'áá ííYiSíí AHéHEé. Thank you very much. There are many people who believe in the spirit of HA'íí'ááGO, Rising Sun. One of them lives six thousand miles away. He is the pope in Rome. And he gave me three gifts, one for each of Rising Sun's miracles…for the light, the mist, and the energy particles."

I paused to drink from a bottle of water.

"The first of these gifts, I gave to the family of my late husband. Today, I would like to give the second gift to my new family, the DiNé or Navajo Nation…in the form of a check made out to the Chinle Clinic so that the healing performed by Rising Sun can continue through the efforts of our new medicine man, Caring Arms…and the physician who brought Rising Sun to Columbus, my dear cousin, Dr. Bill Green. Caring Arms, would you like to read the amount?"

Here was another eye-popping moment. "One million dollars? This can't be a real check!"

"Oh, it is."

And the mammoth gathering responded in kind.

"Tomorrow, I must return home, so I say to all of you once again, thank you and HáGOóNEé. Goodbye."

* * *

We were invited to dinner by Mama Bear, an offer we dared not refuse. We learned that beef, fish, and pork were rarely on a Navajo bill of fare. But the treat today was mutton. I've had rack of lamb before, but never tasted an older sheep. I had other questions for Mama Bear.

"Very nice home…I wasn't sure if perhaps, you would be living in a hogan, the traditional Navajo hut."

"Only a few still do, Phoenix. They're mostly used now for ceremonial purposes. When you've got four kids like mine, they demand their TV shows, so we need electricity."

"Internet?"

"We wish…Some have, but we're still working on it. Hey! Let me introduce you to the rest of my HAK'éi, my family. This is my husband, SHASH Li-CHi, meaning Red Bear…my younger daughter DiBé YAZHí—she's my Little Lamb; she's eleven…and finally my wild child. That's not his name but it probably should be—SHASH YáZHí, eight-year-old Little Bear. If that name sounds familiar, it's because Caring Arms gave it up after his own healing four years ago."

"So it's a hand-me-down name?"

"Oh no, my little guy wanted it like a prized possession, so big brother presented it to him for his sixth birthday…quite a ceremony."

Mama Bear the "chef" then took over. "Listen up, people," she demanded. "We're doing shoulder cuts for dinner, and you should savor every bite, because you won't find better in any restaurant in Arizona. You greenhorns from back east might say it's a little tough and gamey, but don't tell that to Dr. Bill. He'll go around the table and clean off your plates. Let's see if he's been paying attention. Dr. Bill, name me the nine not-so-secret herbs and spices I use to make perfect mutton."

"You're putting me on the spot, but let's try…garlic, olive oil, mint, wine, rosemary, thyme, pepper, dry mustard, and curry powder."

"Impressive, I might even invite you back. You folks make sure you leave room for the corn cake, the beans and squash, pumpkin fry bread, wolfberries, and we'll cut up some watermelon for dessert."

If she'd ask me, I was quite satisfied with the gamey flavor of her prized mutton. I enjoyed having my taste buds attacked, and I took it slow, like a connoisseur, considering each sip from a fine wine.

As we were finishing dessert, Red Bear offered up another invitation. "Tonight at 8:00, every male at this table is welcome to return to the pow-wow and join us in the Tá CHééH, the sweat lodge. Its purpose is to cleanse and purify the body, mind, and spirit…and oddly, it's a tradition we have in common with the Bi CH'AH YAZHi DiNéH'EH, the Jewish people."

"But what do those words mean?" I asked.

"It means 'people who wear little hats.'"

I smiled. "Good description…But the tradition you are speaking of is the 'schvitz?…like a steam bath?"

"Yes, we sing songs, tell stories, talk about future ceremonies."

My mom had heard enough. "Mr. Red Bear, can you please explain why Carli and I are, once again, excluded from this all-boys club?"

"Not true," Red Bear replied. "The women use the sweat lodge during the daytime…it just depends on how soon."

"How soon, what?" Mom asked.

"How soon you want to get naked…Everyone leaves their clothing outside the Tá CHééH upon entering."

Ooooooohh, Mom's face was turning a shade of scarlet any Ohio State Buckeyes fan would recognize, as everyone around the dinner table shared a good laugh.

"Count me in," Dad told Red Bear. "It'll feel just like home."

* * *

But soon once again, we had to say a difficult HáGOóNEé, farewell to good friends. Mama Bear saved her final bear hug for me and said, "I enjoyed cooking for my daughter."

And I got a respectful bow from Caring Arms, who, by rule, was not allowed to touch his sister. "HáGOóNEé."

Bill pulled up his SUV and we proceeded to the last stop on our itinerary, the Chinle cemetery, about a mile north of town. Rising Sun's gravesite was surrounded by a rectangular brick frame one foot tall, which was filled with abundant stacks of flower bouquets.

I read from another of Mama Bear's cards.

"I tell you one idea to keep,
I'm with you still, I do not sleep,
Do not think of me as gone,
I'm with you still, at each new dawn."

MAMA BEAR, RED BEAR, LITTLE BEAR, BLUEBIRD   LITTLE LAMB, CARING ARMS

FIFTEEN

The hotel room door opened at 11:00 a.m. and Mom and I walked into the suite where Dad was just waking up. "Have you already been out this morning?" he asked.

My excitement could not be contained. "Dad! Mama Bear and her girls took us to the sweat lodge, and the other little girls started grabbing my arms and one of them yelled in English, 'Mom, look what I found!' Then they led me to the hot rocks...Did you know that it's really hot in there? So I guess I was their object of attention and they bopped me with their dolls and wanted me to tell THEM a story. So I did the obvious, Phoenix Rising from the Ashes. I had Googled it after I saw the statue."

"Nice side braids too."

"Bluebird started one side, and Little Lamb copied her on the other. I want to come back. It was quite uplifting. Even Mom went in."

Dad scoffed at such a notion, "No, that didn't happen."

Mom shook her head. "Roland, no one says 'no' to Mama Bear."

* * *

The engine of the Piper Saratoga came to life and our cousin gave Dad the signal to push the throttle forward. This time, taking off *was* fun.

"You'll learn to work all the controls today," he told my father. "But first, we're going to do a flyby of the football field since the pow-wow is into its second day."

Sure enough, the big crowd was still there, waving at us and cheering as Bill waggled his wings.

"Great send-off, Bill," I said. "Thanks for escorting us this weekend."

"It was Phoenix Rising who deserves the thanks. You did a terrific job on everything. And Holy Jehoshaphat, a million dollars? I never saw *that* coming. It'll be a godsend to our clinic and the whole Nation...Did you hear that in the middle row? Thank you!"

"You're welcome!" I yelled back.

The hour went by quickly, but Dad was starting to get hooked on flying. He wrenched his neck around. "Laura, honey...We really should buy our own airplane. It's fun. We could fly all over the country any time we wanted to."

Mom was not impressed. "Roland, I've been married to you long enough that I can always tell when you're talking out of your rear end."

For the next two weeks, we relaxed and continued the process of settling into our new home. The crowds had finally dissipated at our old house, so people must have finally gotten the word that we would not be returning. Now we could make our own trips there at 3:00 a.m. without a police escort.

At one point during dinner, I expressed my wishes for the immediate future. "It's time," I said. "I'm not fond of big crowds, but I have an obligation to fulfill."

Mom sighed. "You know it's probably not going to be as much fun as Arizona."

"Fun or not, I'll do what I have to do."

At that, Dad pulled out his cell phone. "I'll call the pope's emissary, the one I met in the ICU conference room."

But I stopped my father in his tracks. "I have his name and number, Dad. This is my obligation." Then I smiled at him. "The pope gave me his card."

In the next minute, I was connected with Monsignor Mateo Romano in Rome. I wasn't sure how many time zones we crossed, but he did answer my call and was pleased with my request.

"Very good, Carli," he responded. "I'll make the arrangements and we will leave in two weeks."

* * *

We departed Cleveland Hopkins Airport on a warm Saturday in a nearly empty plane. Well, aside from us, the pilots, and Monsignor Romano, it *was* empty...a private charter where, for the first time, we could sit in first class. The nine-hour flight gave us plenty of time to chat.

The emissary told us, "His Holiness is quite pleased that you have accepted his invitation to come to Rome."

"This all just seems so imaginary," I replied.

"Have no worries, Carli. You will do fine and I will personally guide you through all of the proceedings. You need only smile and wave your hand very slowly, like the British Royals...Then the three million spectators will love you."

I lost my breath. "Huh? Did you say three million?"

"Yes, at minimum, Carli. There will be 500 thousand in Saint Peter's Square and another two and a half million outside watching on the giant TV screens. But you will be on a covered stage at the Lord's Table. You're not afraid of large crowds, are you?"

"Oh, not at all…not at all," I fibbed just a little. "But why so many people?"

"Carli, proclaiming a living saint is a rare occasion. You are following in the footsteps of Mother Teresa."

"But I can't possibly live up to her."

"Nobody is expecting you to. This is all about your three miracles. A lot of times, people just shrug when they hear of minor miracles. Maybe a person with a tumor prayed to a prospective saint, and their tumor went away. Nobody really understands that or pays much attention. But *everybody* understands *your* miracles, Carli, because yours are the first to have stumped twenty-first century technology. All of the scientists and even all of the world's greatest magicians cannot explain the dynamics of changing third-degree burns into smooth skin. Nor can they begin to explain the vanishing of hardware from your spinal surgery."

I sighed, "I can't either, really."

"You were not made aware that we had fifteen other scientists with us in Columbus. So there were, in total, nineteen representatives of the pontiff. We did not sleep. Each x-ray was examined with a microscope many times. We argued, we debated, we analyzed. There was more research performed on your case in a short period of time than was done for the Shroud of Turin. We called the pope and insisted that he fly to Columbus to meet you. Only *your* miracles are so improbable that they defy the laws of physics. And common people around the world understand that. They see an ordinary human being who, beyond all doubt, has been touched by God."

Our plane landed at Leonardo da Vinci International Airport just outside of Rome. We were met by a small delegation on the tarmac; so, fortunately, we did not need to expose ourselves to the commotion in the terminal. Many travelers had come to Rome for Sunday's big event.

As we were driven to Vatican City in cars with dark-tinted windows, my dad asked, "Can you believe all this? Can you tell me how three nobodies from Ohio could spark worldwide controversy?"

I just waved him off. "You and Mom have the easy jobs on this trip. Just stand in the background and act like proud parents. Do I have to learn Latin now? I was really struggling with Navajo."

"Latin's easy," he told me. "Pretend you're Harry Potter casting a spell."

Upon our arrival at the Vatican, we were assigned two adjoining guest rooms in the Domus Sanctae Marthae (Saint Martha's Guest House) just south of the Basilica. I had the single. Room service came quickly and we had what was considered the pope's favorite dinner…baked chicken, salad, fruit, and wine.

Afterward, Monsignor Romano came by. "I trust your meal was satisfactory?"

"Tasty…very good," I said.

"Carli, if you would follow me now please to the Sacristy building next door, we can get you fitted with a white robe for tomorrow's ceremony."

I followed my host north to the next building where I came upon hundreds of robes and a vast array of religious uniforms.

"The pontiff has his own changing room, Carli. For you, here, try this robe on…simple, plain, and white."

I thanked my host and went to change. When we returned to our suite, my parents were watching a well-dressed TV news anchor exclaim, "Carli Green e burlare di secolo!" (Carli Green is the hoax of the century!)

Monsignor Romano interpreted for us. "The man said 'Carli Green is most welcome in our city.'"

My parents were a bit curious as to why my full length robe was so plain and featureless.

"We are following in the humble tradition of Mother Teresa," our host explained. "We are not coronating a queen. After tomorrow's brief ceremony, the real work begins—allowing the sick and the lame to touch your hand. Carli Green, do you feel up to the task?"

I was resolute. "Yes sir, that is the reason why I have come to Rome."

The monsignor then presented me with a thin chain necklace and he fastened it around my neck. "A gift from His Holiness."

I'm not sure why I was surprised. "A Star of David, really?"

He reminded me, "When you met the pope in Columbus, did he not mention his sensitivity regarding the Inquisition?"

"He did."

"In 1492, the Jewish population of Spain was given an edict…to accept forced conversion, deportation, or death. The pontiff wants to make certain that you understand that tomorrow's ceremony is not a conversion…and you may keep the chain."

I slightly bowed my head. "Please tell His Holiness that I appreciate both his concern and his generosity."

Monsignor Romano repeated a slight bow and departed.

I shook my head. "Wow, so this is really happening."

* * *

We arose at 8:00 a.m. Sunday and breakfast was brought to our rooms. My parents dressed in the best attire that they could find at home and we nervously awaited the instructions to proceed to the 10:00 a.m. service.

In my plain white robe, I was the calmest of all of us. I felt that my experience in the Navajo Nation gave me greater confidence. If I could become Phoenix Rising, then I could also become Saint Carli.

Monsignor Romano knocked on our door at 9:50, cutting it really close. Dad asked me, "Are you okay, kiddo?"

I grabbed his hand and smiled at him. "Relax, Dad. Everything will be fine."

We followed the emissary's lead, taking us north through the Sacristy and into the main structure, Saint Peter's Basilica.

"Today's ceremony will be much shorter," our escort explained, "because as a living person, Carli cannot be fully canonized."

A few hundred steps later, we faced a heavy bronze door that served as one of the main entrances to the Basilica. Split in half vertically, it was opened for us by two members of the colorful Swiss Guard.

Monsignor Romano wasted no time. He pointed, palm up, and invited us to proceed through the door with me in the lead. Almost instantly, a sea of people erupted into a thunderous ovation. It took my eyes several seconds to make an adjustment to the brilliant sunshine. But now I believed the reports that a half million people could be shoehorned into Saint Peter's Square. It was overwhelming to say the least.

The pope was standing right next to us. I would have to say that he looked quite different without his Buckeye gear. He now wore the traditional white cassock robe, the mozzetta cape, satin sash, and the same zucchetto cap I had seen him wear in Columbus.

"Welcome," he said to us with a nod and a smile.

We each returned the greeting with the words, "Your Holiness."

We weren't expecting him to extend a hand but he did. Were we allowed to shake hands with a pope? I didn't know. We just followed his lead. Then we were split up. Mom and Dad were directed left to sit in the side-facing front row of the VIP section. Opposite them were cardinals in red zucchettos and bishops in violet.

I was asked to stand next to the pope in front of the papal throne, a white

99

chair placed on a raised stage, and under a red canopy. The image above us must have produced quite a wow factor for Mom and Dad…a ten-foot-high banner of my face…but from my vertical angle, I could barely recognize it.

One hundred feet in front of us was the Lord's Table, a long white table with a bronze front that also had a raised stage and canopy. The monsignor had told me that this was where the "main events" would occur.

With a signal given, the Sistine Chapel Choir, composed of both men and boys, began their hymns as families with children came forward to place religious relics on or near the Lord's Table. A gold Bible and chalice were presented to the pope.

After some preliminary speakers, the pope rose to address the audience from in front of the papal throne. He asked all to be seated, and I sat on a velvet stool next to the throne. I couldn't see above his lectern but I assumed he was reading from the gold Bible…and he continued reading for about fifteen minutes.

Then he pointed the way for me to follow him down the steps to the Lord's Table. The event was moving at a pretty rapid clip. Other dignitaries joined us. But all I could think of was, "Don't trip on the robe!"

One of the priests then placed the mitre, the pointed ceremonial head-gear, upon the pope's head. Others swung chained thuribles to distribute burning incense.

When the pope started speaking again, this time in Latin, I could feel my knees rattling just a little.

I struggled to comprehend any of the pope's Latin. Then I realized that Monsignor Romano stood behind me ready to offer the English translation.

"DEUS SUUM AMOREM DAT OMNIBUS."

"God gives his love to all of us."

"HAEC MULIERI TANGITUR A DEO."

"This woman is touched by God."

"ERGO ANNUNTIO ILLI TRIA MIRACULA."

"Therefore I proclaim those three miracles."

"ERGO BENEDICAT HUIC MULIERI CARLI GREEN."

"Therefore I will bless this woman Carli Green."

"ERGO ANNUNTIO VIVENS SANC."

"Therefore I proclaim the living saint."

"SANC CARLI DE COLUMBUS."

"Saint Carli of Columbus."

"PATRONUS DE BUCKEYES."

"Patron Saint of Buckeyes."

I had to cover my ears for a most thunderous ovation that followed. Three million voices approved the proclamation.

I figured that maybe four or five spectators among the millions here knew what a Buckeye was.

Boldly, and nervously, I asked for permission to use the microphone.

I cleared my throat. "My first act is to donate one of my miracles, one million dollars, to be shared by the homeless shelter, Palazo Migliori, and by the Gemelli Hospital which serves the poor. Grazie…Thank you."

Upon regaining the microphone, the pope repeated my pledge in Italian, generating another great round of applause. He shook hands with me again, and the ceremony was complete.

The pope's emissary then escorted the three of us back to our guest quarters. My dad commented, "I remembered that years ago when Laura and I got married, the ceremony was followed by a noisy reception line, hors d'oeuvres, open bar, dancing…There was none of that today."

Monsignor Romano spoke plainly. "Lunch will be brought up shortly. Saint Carli, you performed well today. The people appreciate your humility and generosity. There are also some gifts for you in the suitcase in the corner. When would you like to start working?"

I was eager. "Right after lunch, sir."

"Excellent. You'll be meeting guests in the Sistine Chapel, and your parents are welcome to sit nearby."

We all thanked him. Then I ran to open the suitcase.

"Wow, the pope was right. They put my face on everything…mugs, T-shirts, dinner plates, key chains…they've even got your refrigerator magnets, Dad."

"Except your compensation is gone," he told me. "Mom and I thought that you might at least keep some for your own living expenses."

"Dad, haven't you heard of 'NIL'…name, image, likeness? There's never been a Patron Saint of Buckeyes before. They'll probably sell zillions of these in Columbus."

"That sounds great, Carli. Except first, we must give thanks to the pope for sending us pizza for lunch."

* * *

Two hours later, the Monsignor returned with our instructions.

"You will be seated at the front end of the Sistine Chapel. Mr. and Mrs. Green, you will sit off to the side. Saint Carli, one at a time, each family will approach you, and you will extend your bare right hand for the afflicted person to touch. Do not leave your seat and do not show any emotion. The people who touch you will be EXTREMELY emotional. We anticipate perhaps one in ten will faint. Even though you view yourself as an ordinary person, these people believe that touching you is the closest they will ever come to touching God."

"How many families will I be meeting?" I asked.

"Twenty-three thousand."

I smacked the side of my face. "Seriously?!"

"You'll recall that the pope asked you to take a sabbatical of thirty days. It will actually be six days per week for four weeks. So 24 days times 8 hours times 60 minutes times 2 families per minute equals 23,040…with time of course for meals and bathroom breaks."

"Isn't thirty seconds per family awfully quick?"

"It will be time enough for our official photographer to take their picture while touching your hand. A lottery was held earlier to select the attending families. Otherwise, three million worshipers would make for a very long line. But of those who touch you, none will want to leave. So we will have some assistants to keep the line moving. Will you agree to this schedule?"

As at the Sandwich Condo, I didn't complain about my duties. "Yes, of course I will."

"Excellent. One other thing, most of these people will have some type of illness. Everyone, including you, must wear a face mask at all times, even for photographs. When each party leaves, an altar boy will wash your right hand with a moist towel. Do you have any questions?"

"No sir."

"Then let us proceed."

We retraced our earlier path. I was still lost, but we returned north through the Sacristy and the Basilica. In a few minutes, we were led to the magnificently decorated chamber of the Sistine Chapel. There was nothing like it in the world…one of the greatest works by the master painter and sculptor Michelangelo. I looked up to see the famous panel of the *Creation of Adam*. I guess this is where everyone got the idea that God is an old guy with a long white beard.

Still wearing my plain white robe, I was seated near the front in an

Sistine Chapel

ordinary chair, but below the altar. Obviously, they couldn't have people in wheelchairs struggling up the four steps.

The families were lined up along the left side wall and my folks were given seats on the right. When the first family was signaled to approach, it didn't take long for the fireworks to start.

A woman approached, pushing her husband in a wheelchair. She grabbed the man's hand, then grabbed my hand, clamping them together in a mighty squeeze…but she wouldn't let go. Then she started screaming, "Oh Dio! Oh Dio! Guariscilo Ora!" (Oh God! Heal it now!)

I tugged back, but was unable to free my right hand. Four large men approached. Technically, they were Vatican assistants, but could be more accurately described as the pope's "bouncers."

The woman screamed even louder (OH DIO!) as she sprawled on the floor and latched on to my left leg.

Two of the men grabbed her right arm and two, her left. With effort, they extricated the worshipper while an altar boy wheeled her husband to the exit.

I thought, "That went well. So if my math is correct, that's one down and 23,039 to go. Didn't that little boy Jimmy do the exact same thing to me back in Columbus?"

The experiences with the next four parties did not go much better. I looked at Monsignor Romano and placed my hands in a 'T' formation, signaling that I wanted a time-out.

"This isn't working for me," I told him. "I'm throwing out the rule book!"

"Saint Carli, what do you mean?" he asked with alarm.

"I can't just sit there like a lump! In the sandwich shop, people picked up on my body language. Their faces brightened when they noticed that I actually cared about my customers. And the mask has to go. My smile is everything. My smile disarms people. It's time to use some mojo."

Not waiting for his response, I started "chatting up" the altar boy, the one with the wash cloth. Nodding his head, he apparently was catching on to what I had in mind.

Then I whirled my index finger in circle indicating "Let's get the show on the road here."

The next party to come forward brought with them a sick child. I could not even tell if the child was a boy or girl. Playing my role of Saint Carli, I got off the chair and stooped down to be at eye level with the child. I clasped the child's hands with both of my own hands. Then I spoke the Italian words I was searching for…while displaying my killer smile of course.

"BENVENUTO MIO FIGLIO, DIO TI AMA." (Welcome, my child. God loves you.)

The faces of the child and the parents absolutely lit up. I had asked if the thumbs-up sign was approved by the Church and it was. It made for a perfect shot by the photographer and a great souvenir for this family.

Then I pointed to the exit door and said firmly, "ANDARE CON DIO." (Go with God)…and every single person after that nodded and obeyed this command. After all, who would dare have the nerve to say no to a saint?

* * *

I was on a roll. I locked myself into "sandwich shop girl" mode, and it was no different than spending all day greeting customers. For me, it didn't feel like work anymore.

On my off-days, the Vatican was more than happy to take us touring to places like Florence, Pisa, and Pompeii, the ancient city destroyed by Mt. Vesuvius. And we had a chance to visit the Coliseum in Rome nearby. Our black-wig disguises worked well and nobody bothered us. No one pointed at us and said, "Hey, there goes Groucho Marx."

I also encouraged my parents to tour the streets on my workdays and stop at some nice restaurants. There was no reason for them to sit at my repetitive sessions in the Sistine Chapel.

It took me five weeks, not four, to reach lottery number 23,040 but I stayed the course to the last family and fulfilled my commitment. We all happily started packing to leave.

"So, Dad," I spoke up, "what am I supposed to do since my full name is now 'Carli Green Cassie Johnson Phoenix Rising Saint Carli of Columbus Patron Saint of Buckeyes?'"

"Impressive," he replied. "I don't believe anyone's ever had a moniker quite like that. Pray that no one asks you for an autograph."

"But what if I don't *want* to be famous? What if I want to go back to being a sandwich shop girl?"

He held my shoulders. "Kiddo, you can be anything you want."

* * *

In the morning after breakfast, we heard a knock at our door and expected Monsignor Romano to begin escorting us to the airport. But it was not him. It was instead, the pope.

"Saint Carli," he said, "you are a worthy saint." He gave me a light hug. "But Monsignor Romano tells me you do not follow the rules."

"I'm sorry, Your Holiness, but—"

"No, no, no," he interrupted. "We have changed the name of the rules to the 'Saint Carli rules'...Andare con Dio," he said to us all.

And we all returned, "Andare con Dio."

SIXTEEN

The next few weeks had all three of us searching for new routines to keep us busy. Watching TV wasn't one of them. It seemed that the Navajo Event had replaced Sasquatch as the world's most popular conspiracy theory. Mom and Dad had to quit their jobs and we wore our black wigs pretty much all the time…except when visiting the grandparents. Every news and cable network wanted to interview us but, I'm sorry, we had no interest in talking to them about the "hoax of the century."

Mom resumed her old hobby of sewing doll clothes and also volunteered calling Bingo at the local senior center. Dad got into books and movies and started training to become a substitute teacher. We all took walks together every evening.

I was, however, still restless, and did something my parents figured was unthinkable. I applied for and was hired on as Cassie Johnson at one of the local franchises of the Sandwich Condo. I could now say that The Patron Saint of Buckeyes was happy again. To top it off, I purchased a beagle puppy from a local rescue center and named her Lucy, sticking with the influence of the *Peanuts* gang.

I really thought we were done with our extended fifteen minutes of fame…until one day, my cell phone rang and I didn't recognize the number. Who knew the Johnsons?

"Hello."

"Is that you, Carli?"

"I'm sorry, this is Cassie Johnson. You must have the wrong number. Goodbye."

"Carli, wait! It's Gerald Zimblist from the FBI."

I wasn't sure how to react. "Okay…Is this good news or bad news?"

"I'm not certain, but first I want to congratulate you for a job well done in Rome."

"Thank you, Mr. Zimblist. So what's the uncertain news for me?"

"Carli, I received a call earlier today from a woman with whom I've worked well in the past. Her name is Mandy Aurora and she's kind of a psychic."

"Mr. Zimblist, my interest in talking to a psychic about the Navajo Event lies somewhere between zero and none."

"You might want to change your mind about this one, Carli. She's good.

She reads auras and she helped me solve a case once, when all our technology couldn't."

"So why did she wait till now to call?"

"Mandy prefers to stay out of the limelight. She's a schoolteacher in Canton and wants no part of the fortune-telling business. As for her talent, she works privately for no pay and only gets involved if the subject interests her."

"As far as I'm concerned, the subject is over. Why should I call her now?"

"Curiosity if nothing else. There's no guarantee, but I think she might be able to tell you things that no one else could…and she'll keep everything in the strictest confidence. I would do it myself except the FBI is no longer on the case. Look, just write down her number and decide later if you want to call. I can't force you. Okay?"

"Fine."

* * *

I waited a day, but Mr. Zimblist was right. Curiosity was getting the better of me, and I picked up the phone.

"Hello," she answered.

"Is this Mandy Aurora?"

"Yes it is."

"This is Carli Green. Agent Zimblist said that you wanted to speak with me?"

The woman practically exploded in her excitement. "OH, HI CARLI! I am so, so, so happy you called me! We need to get together."

"Really? Why?"

"Because I might be able to help explain *the* Event. But let me first explain to you that I got this rhyming nick name when I was in high school and I'm stuck with it. I own it. My name is Mandy Aurora who sees all the auras."

"Cute, but why didn't you come to Columbus during the investigation when we had all the big name magicians in town?"

"Because those are entertainers. I have tremendous respect for their profession, and they are all very talented. But tell me this, Carli. If the Navajo Event were really a hoax, shouldn't at least one of all those brilliant magicians have been able to figure it out?"

"They didn't because it wasn't a hoax."

"Exactly! I deal strictly with science. Sure, I could have made a comfortable living doing pseudo-science…telling people that their auras dictated their moods or their futures. It would have been far more lucrative than astrology or teaching. But I had the calling to be an elementary school teacher and I love my decision. And by the way, kids have the best auras—so much energy."

"So what exactly are the auras? Some kind of strange light above your head?"

"It's not so strange, Carli. All living things, and some non-living things, give off electromagnetic energy. It's one of the four major forces of the universe. When viewed through high-voltage cameras, as in Kirlian photography, the auras appear as light emanating from your body. You've driven under power lines before, haven't you? What happens to your radio then?"

"It crackles."

"Right, and that proves that even though you can't see the energy, you know it's there. Every human is a walking radio station broadcasting electromagnetic signals. But some humans emit tremendously more energy than others. And when that happens, it can permanently impress an image onto a nearby solid surface. It's not that much different from exposing photo paper in an old time darkroom."

"Are you sure about that?"

"Carli, look at the Shroud of Turin. It's the world's most famous aura. Whether or not it was really Jesus, I don't know. But whoever this person was, he emitted a fantastic amount of energy, and his image became etched into the cloth, just like a photographic negative."

"Did you tell the scientists it was an aura?"

"I tried to, but they dismissed me as a psychic kook. That's why I don't go public anymore."

"So you want to go to the room where the healing ceremony took place and see if the medicine man left something like the Shroud of Turin etched on the wall?"

"You're catching on, Carli."

"Mandy, I don't understand how you can see these things."

"You can call it either a gift or a curse. But I don't have a choice. When you open your eyes, do you see in color?"

"Yes."

"Always? Or do you have a choice to turn off your 'gift' and see the world in black and white?"

"I have no choice. I always see in color."

"And I always see auras, everywhere and all the time. But it is my experience that regardless of color or layering, in most cases, auras do not affect or reveal characteristics of one's personality. And that's why everyone in the 'aura business' hates me. But…there can be some exceptions for high-energy people."

"Can you sense my aura right now?"

"Only when I see you in person. Hey, did you know that Ted Williams, the great baseball player, had 20/10 vision? It was the best eyesight of any human. It was a gift. Unfortunately, my gift doesn't help me hit home runs, but I'm not complaining."

"So what exactly is your plan, Mandy?"

"I'm off tomorrow. We meet at the medical center at noon. You lead us up to your room in the ICU, I look at the walls, and we're out of there."

I took a deep breath. "Mandy, it's just not that easy. For one thing, there's a reception desk in the ICU that we'd have to get past. Another thing…If the department head, Dr. Dred, sees me, she will probably have me arrested."

"Zimblist said you guys all have black wigs, right?"

"Yes."

"Okay, and I have two white lab coats. I've snuck into hospitals before, and they don't know me at Ohio State. I'll also bring my laptop computer and a stethoscope. You just bring your wig and a clipboard with pretend medical papers on it."

"Have you ever shared a jail cell with anyone before?"

"Come on, Carli. Where's your sense of adventure? It's easy. You just walk quickly with a purpose and keep your head down. We pretend that we're pointing at the other person's notes. And I quietly say stuff to you like 'What do you think of the second procedure going forward?' And then you say something like 'We should probably go back and re-check the test results before making a decision.' Carli, if you walk confidently, I promise no one will question you."

"You know I was asleep during the Navajo Event."

"Maybe so, but tomorrow, you'll be wide awake."

* * *

I told my parents I was driving to Columbus on the premise that I was visiting Libby. But I was concerned that today's real mission had a good amount of danger to it.

Leaving at 10:00 a.m., I arrived on time at noon in front of the hospital,

110

clipboard in hand, where previously, fifty-thousand angry news junkies demanded answers to explain the Navajo Event. Now, Mandy and I were doing the same. She saw me and waved.

"Did you recognize me by my aura?" I asked her.

"No, Carli. I recognized you because your face has been in the news for months. And you'll be relieved to know that you do have an aura."

Mandy definitely could pass for the schoolmarm type…a bit on the portly side, glasses, hair in a bun, and a nice smile. I hoped she could pass for a doctor too. She looked good in her lab coat and stethoscope.

"Are you ready to do this, Carli?"

"Not really, but I guess there's no turning back now."

"Take this bag and try the coat on in the women's room, but don't let anyone see you. I'll hold your clipboard."

When I returned, she gave me her approval. "Dr. Jones, I think you'll pass muster."

I peeked at her name tag. "Dr. Brown, I believe we'll make a great team. Time to head up to the sixth floor."

We stepped onto the first empty elevator. I pressed six and the doors began closing. But a hand suddenly banged the edge of one door…and in stepped Dr. Logan Duncan, crocodile hunter.

He tipped his safari hat in a polite gesture. "G'day," he said.

Mandy didn't know it, but I thought my heart was about to explode out of my chest. If anything went wrong, this doctor would personally escort us to a cell on the eighth-floor prison ward. For a second, I wondered if he had replaced the hunting knife he had given my dad. Thankfully, at least, he pressed five.

It took seemingly forever to get to the fifth floor, but when we got there, he simply walked off and I exhaled.

"Who was *that* guy?" Mandy asked. "He's a live wire. His aura was so strong, it was bouncing off all four walls of the elevator. I had to close my eyes. It was driving me crazy."

"That, Mandy, was my spinal surgeon. I thought for sure he'd nail us."

"No worries, Carli. This place has over sixteen thousand employees. I looked it up. The numbers are on our side."

Mandy and I arrived at the sixth floor, and we stepped off. "Remember the plan, Carli. We act quick and confident, then we make our move."

When we entered the ICU lobby, my worst fears were realized. Dr. Dred was conversing with the receptionists. Mandy picked up on her energy signature right away.

"Who's that one with the 'prickly' aura? That's nasty. She's like fingernails on a chalkboard, only for eyes instead of ears. Is that your infamous Dr. Dred?"

"I have to say you're good, Mandy."

"Oh? You believe in wizards now? Look, a party of five family members is being let in. We can blend in, right in the middle."

Using that family as a shield, we kept our faces turned away from Dr. Dred and passed through the "gate" undetected.

"Pick up the pace, Carli. Which one was your room?"

"Room 8 at the end."

This hallway was not a place of fond memories. Often, I wished we could just turn back the clock and not have the fire ever happen.

The door to room 8 was partially open and no one was inside except a patient, an elderly woman in bed. Mandy boldly entered and walked directly up to the patient asking, "And how are we doing today?"

While the patient tried to answer, Mandy scanned the walls of the room and issued me an order. "Draw the hanging curtain all the way back."

I did.

"AAAAGGGGHHHH!!! Ooooooooooooohhhhhhhh."

I rushed to Mandy's side. "What happened?"

She moaned loudly. "Carli, I just looked at the sun and I'm temporarily blinded. Take my hand and get us out of here fast!"

Several nurses heard her screams and came running to room 8, but I rushed past them, saying, "Everything's fine."

I was absolutely determined to get us out of the ICU and was willing to brush by or bowl over any person who got in the way. No one tried to stop the two running doctors, although a few medical personnel asked, "Is anything wrong?" I replied, "Everything's fine," and continued forward through the ICU lobby and into the corridor. I wasn't about to wait for an elevator. I led Mandy down the stairs to the fourth floor. (The fifth had Dr. Duncan.)

From there, we grabbed an elevator and exited the building through the front door where we came in. I asked, "Are you okay? And how did you manage to hold on to your laptop?"

She blinked several times and wiped her eyes. "There are still some spots in front of my eyes, but it's a little better…and I'm a teacher. I can't afford to drop my laptop."

"So what happened back there, Mandy?"

"I accidentally looked at the sun."

"But why would you look out the window? I thought you were just going to look at walls."

Mandy took a deep breath. "Carli, I *was* looking at the wall. It was like seeing a billion auras. Didn't *you* see the sun?"

"No, I didn't see a bright light of any kind."

"Wow, Carli…Something seriously whacked out happened in that room."

"I could have told you that, and I'm not even a psychic."

She shook her head. "Carli, can we go someplace quiet and talk?"

"I know just the place."

* * *

We entered the Sandwich Condo where I used to work. Since none of my co-workers recognized me in the wig, we ordered two tuna-melts and grabbed a booth in the back.

"First of all, Mandy, how are your eyes?"

"They're better. The spots are going away, but still, that never happened before. Nothing should have an aura as bright as the sun."

"But something did."

Mandy leaned forward to whisper. "Carli, your dad was in the room during the healing ceremony. Did he say what the medicine man was doing? Was he sitting, standing, jumping, twirling—?"

"Dad told me he was standing…with both hands over his heart."

"Are you sure it was his heart?"

"Who knows? Weren't they all wearing gowns?"

She put a hand on her chin in thought. "Is the security camera footage from the news still on YouTube…the part that shows the Navajo folks walking through the ICU hallway?"

Mandy didn't wait for me to answer. She opened her laptop and typed in the desired search parameter, and then clicked "play."

So there they were…Bill and the four Navajos.

Mandy hit the pause button. "Look at *that*, Carli…the pendant around Rising Sun's neck. Do you know anything about that?"

"Yes, it's the pendant that I used to anoint Rising Sun's successor, Caring Arms. That's the young man you see on your screen."

"Okay, but did they ever say any more about it…like what the purpose was for the jewels or the rectangular black stone in the middle?"

"My cousin, Dr. Bill Green, told me that there was a legend that the healing powers of the pendant had been passed down through many generations of medicine men…but that no one knows how it was started."

"Is that it?"

"There's more. When we went to Arizona, Caring Arms said to me, 'I am nothing without the pendant, and only the spirit of my predecessor can transfer the power of the pendant.'"

That put Mandy into deep thought. "Hmm…okay…So everyone thinks that the pendant is special, and I just saw an aura that looks like the sun… Did they say if it was the jewels or the black stone that was special?"

"Bill said the black stone was called the healing stone."

"And when were you going to tell me that, next week?"

I shrugged.

"Okay, you said that Rising Sun had his hands over his heart. Could he have actually been placing his hands over the black stone instead?"

"He could have, I suppose."

"Hmm…Okay, so the black stone looks like it has a shape similar to a small box that would hold a pack of playing cards. Carli, I would like to know the exact dimensions of that stone. Is there a way that you could find that out for me?"

"I think so. I've got Bill's number…and he said he works with Caring Arms at the clinic."

"Great. Give him a call right now."

I wasn't sure what Mandy was getting at, but she sure seemed to have the nose of a detective.

"Hey, Bill, this is your cousin Carli."

"Good to hear from you again. There's still a big buzz around the Navajo Nation. 'Phoenix Rising mania' hasn't diminished. And we all loved watching you on TV from Rome. So what's up with you?"

"I was wondering if you could do me a small favor. Just for curiosity's sake, could you please measure the length, width, and depth of the black stone on Caring Arm's pendant?"

There was silence for five seconds. I thought the line had gone dead. "Bill?"

Then a loud screech sounded like he was trying to pass a kidney stone.

"Carli, do you remember me telling you that it was bad karma to question good fortune and that we should just leave it alone?!"

"I do, yes."

"Then why are you questioning good fortune *now*?"

"I'll be totally honest with you, Bill. I'm working with a person who reads auras who says that the pendant has the aura of the sun."

"That's cool, Carli...So now you've joined a 'wizards and warlocks' gang bent on acquiring the power of the sun?"

"No, Bill. She's a school teacher, and both of us are extremely trustworthy. I absolutely swear to you that we will not take any action with information that you might give us today."

"And does the schoolteacher so swear?"

"I do, Dr. Green," Mandy said into my phone. "I do so swear."

"What is it you want?"

Mandy took my phone. "I'd like the exact dimensions of the black stone as accurately as possible, down to the tenth of a millimeter."

"I see...Well, hold on a sec...Caring Arms is with me now. I'll use a micrometer."

I whispered to Mandy, "Why do you need this?"

She 'shushed' me with an index finger by her lips.

Bill came back on the line. "Okay, mark these down...The length is 126.9 millimeters...The width is 56.4 millimeters...and the depth is 14.1 millimeters."

"Thank you, Dr. Green. We really appreciate it," said Mandy.

"Well, don't you two do anything stupid. Do I make myself clear?"

"Yes, sir," Mandy replied.

"Yes, Bill."

"And Carli, congratulations on everything."

"Thanks, Bill."

"Bye."

"So, Mandy," I said. "Can you tell me now why you needed these measurements?"

"Hold on just a second, Carli...Hmm...hmm...Okay, bingo."

"What have you got?" I eagerly asked her.

"Carli, are you familiar with Arthur C. Clarke's most famous science fiction work?"

"I assume you're talking about *2001 A Space Odyssey*...Yes, I've seen the movie and read the book."

"Well, it's classified as science fiction…but what if it wasn't fiction?"

"Huh? I don't follow."

"Well, the outer space scenes were fictional, but what if the black monoliths were real and he just never told anyone about it?"

"I still don't follow."

"Do the math, Carli. One squared is one. Two squared is four. And three squared is nine. All the black monoliths had a ratio with the depth being one, the width being four, and the length being nine. 1:4:9. Okay, now use the calculator on my laptop. What's 56.4 divided by 14.1?"

"It's four…exactly four."

"And what's 126.9 divided by 14.1?"

"Exactly nine…but Mandy, that's—"

"Don't say 'impossible,' Carli, because that's what everyone's been calling the Navajo Event since the day it happened. So did Rising Sun maybe use a mini black monolith to heal you? I don't know. But aren't those stone blocks supposed to have the power to advance life or even create life?"

I spread my hands apart. "So what do you want me to do now, Mandy… call up the pope and tell him that God doesn't exist? He specifically said that any healing done by advanced aliens could not be considered miracles."

"No, no, no…Come on, Carli. God is still on the playing field here. If advanced beings created the monoliths, then the follow-up question becomes 'Who created the advanced beings?' Even Albert Einstein referred to God as 'The Old One.' So who's to say science and religion can't coexist? Do you have a contact at the Vatican?"

"Yes, it's Monsignor Romano."

"Well, suppose you call up this Romano fella right now and tell him, 'Hey, bro! Guess what! I just met this crazy psycho kook lady who says that I wasn't healed by God at all. That's right! I was actually healed by aliens from outer space!'…Now what do you think your buddy would say to that?"

"Nothing. He would just hang up."

"Right, so your conscience is clear. And what we speculated on today is just a guess anyway. We have no proof…Why don't you answer your phone, Carli?"

Lost in thought, I had been ignoring the rings. "Hello?"

"Miss Johnson?"

"Yes."

"This is Dr. Kline, your new dentist. There seems to be some confusion with the records that you gave me from your previous dentist. And I was wondering if you might be able to help me clear it up."

"Go ahead."

"Well, for one thing, I don't see any fillings or crowns in your mouth that were noted in your past records. But the stranger part is that all four of your wisdom teeth look just fine, and yet your file says they've all been pulled. In fact, this is the first time I've ever come across a person with thirty-two beautifully perfect teeth."

"A patient like that could be bad for business, Dr. Kline."

"Oh, no…On the contrary, when others see your beautiful full set of teeth, they'll assume I do excellent work…which I do of course."

"Well, Dr. Kline, obviously there's been a mix-up and you received the wrong records. I've always been one of the lucky ones with a great smile, and if you just want to start a new file for me, that would be fine."

"That would be fine on my side too, Miss Johnson. Thanks for your help."

"You're most welcome. Bye."

I looked at Mandy. "I never paid much attention to my teeth getting fixed."

"Do you think it happened during the healing ceremony?"

"It had to," I agreed. But then I started laughing about it. "Who in the world would want their wisdom teeth back?"

"Do you suppose there are any *more* surprises for you?"

"Maybe…This could be the gift that keeps on giving."

SEVENTEEN

The next two months passed by pleasantly. Dad acquired a license to be a substitute teacher, and as long as no one recognized him, he found it enjoyable going in and working with the students a few days a week... although one middle-schooler told him he had a bad toupee. That wasn't nice.

Mom and I had no complaints either, and our best outings were when we could ditch the disguises and visit the grandparents' homes for dinner. Those were the only times when we still watched TV, and it seemed that Bigfoot, UFO's, and the Navajo Event became a notable threesome on all the talk shows.

But I really wanted to 'upchuck' each time I saw Drs. Dred and Duncan raking in lots of cash by plying the latest hoax theory (all of which had been debunked by Dr. Stanton and the FBI) to any show that would have them on. Duncan now carried an even bigger hunting knife than the one he gave Dad, and he insisted that I had to be the first human clone. Dred was her same bubbly self, constantly bragging, "I was the one who put Carli Green behind bars."

Oh, how I hated our fifteen minutes of fame.

* * *

As Dad had said, telephone bells at 7:30 a.m. rarely bring good news. It was Sunday morning. I reached for my cell phone on the nightstand. "Who's there?" I mumbled.

"The pope has been shot."

"WHAT? MOM! DAD!" I quickly hit the speakerphone button and ran into my parents' bedroom. "Who is this?"

"Forgive me for disturbing you at your early hour. This is Monsignor Mateo Romano. I will speak bluntly. An hour ago, the pope was shot twice by sniper fire as he was standing in his window delivering Sunday's noon mass. He does not use bulletproof glass. He has serious internal injuries to his heart, lungs, and liver and has been taken to Gemelli Hospital...but is not expected to survive more than six or seven hours. A priest is giving last rites. He is conscious for now, and his final request was to touch the hand of Saint Carli, the hand that was touched by God."

I tried to think straight, shaking the cobwebs from my head. How could I respond?

Monsignor Romano did not wait for my reply. "Saint Carli, a prepaid charter flight is waiting for your family at Cleveland Hopkins Airport. We are fully aware that this nonstop flight would take nine hours to reach Rome. With driving time, you would arrive at the pope's bedside in eleven hours, four hours after he has passed. Therefore, if you choose not to take the flight, no one will think the less of you and no one will know. As the pope's emissary, it was my obligation to pass along the message. Andare con Dio."

-click-

Mom said, "I think we should go. Let's pack our bags."

"NO!" I yelled.

She looked at me with puzzlement. "Excuse me?"

I stood with my hands on hips and stated, "I'm not leaving without my brother."

"Excuse me again?"

"Caring Arms can heal the pope...just like Rising Sun healed me."

Thinking out loud Dad said, "If Bill flew him to Phoenix in an hour, then Phoenix to Rome nonstop would be nine plus four more, that's thirteen hours...so a total of fifteen hours to the pope's bedside." He sighed. "Kiddo, the math doesn't work for us."

Mom asked, "Isn't there any way we can get him there faster?"

Dad shook his head. "I don't know, but even if we could, how do we know that he'd be willing to go?"

"Why wouldn't he?" I asked.

"Because you were the first Caucasian to receive a Navajo healing ceremony. Wouldn't it seem very arrogant on our part to ask for another? Do you think Blue Wolf and the Navajo Nation Council would agree to help a man of the Church after what Cortes and Pizarro did to Native Americans?"

I argued, "But this is the man who gave them a million dollars to help their clinic."

"No, *you* were the one who made that donation."

"Then I should be the one to make the request. I want to call Caring Arms now."

"I don't have his number."

"Then give me Bill's number...please."

My dad exhaled deeply and replied, "Okay."

I wondered what Bill thought of telephone bells at 7:30 in the morning…except where he lived, it was 5:30…great, even better.

He did not answer with a standard greeting of "hello" and he did not sound very happy. "Carli! Tell me you did NOT do something really, really stupid with the info I gave you about the stone! Tell me an electro-magnetic pulse is NOT going to wipe out the national grid!"

"Bill, the pope's been shot."

He exhaled. "I'm sorry to hear that…but I feel that there's more to your call than that."

"I'd like to ask Caring Arms to come with me to Rome to perform a healing ceremony on the pope before he dies."

"Wow…well, to be honest with you, Carli, I think you'd have a better chance asking for your million dollars back. The council will laugh in your face…And at 5:45 a.m., they will grumble loudly in your face, just like I did."

"I still have to try."

"Look, Carli, I understand that this is a serious matter and can't wait. I'm going to drive over to Mama Bear's house right now and hash this out in person, and get you an answer from the council one way or another as soon as possible."

"That's all I ask for…thank you."

* * *

After thirty minutes, my cell phone rang again. I could hear a lot of commotion on the other end. "Yes, Bill?"

"I've got the whole Bear family awake now and I've put a call through to Blue Wolf asking for an emergency session of the council. He understands how serious this matter is…and it's not that they dislike the pope. They just want to follow tribal law. Do you have a laptop available?"

"I do."

"I'm sending a link to your email. Blue Wolf and a number of delegates have Internet and we're setting up a remote session. You can go ahead and enter the room."

"Okay…waiting…waiting…Okay, I'm in."

The three of us watched the screen as names and faces started popping into the room. Blue Wolf and ten of the twenty-four delegates had entered. Bill and Caring Arms occupied one square.

Blue Wolf started the meeting. "We will not waste time on this matter.

If you know of any good reason why a Navajo healing ceremony should be performed on an outsider, then speak your piece now."

I immediately took the floor. "This man, this pope, believed in the spirit of Rising Sun. Before any information hit the news media, he flew to Columbus, Ohio to tell me in person that the miracles performed by this medicine man were channeled through him directly by the supreme beings, the DIYIN DiNé'E. And he told me that the deeds of his predecessors like Cortes and Pizarro have left dark pages in the history books from which we must emerge. He knew that I would pass along a donation to Rising Sun's people. He just didn't want it to appear as though he were patronizing the DiNé. He absolutely believed in the goodness and good deeds of HA'íí'ááGO, Rising Sun. He helped all of us. Now we must help him."

Blue Wolf answered her. "Phoenix Rising, we understand the close relationship you have with the pope, but the healing ceremony is a DiNé affair. If we try to heal one BiLAGáANA (Caucasian) such as yourself, then thousands more will want the same. You saw how they descended on the Nation like a horde of locusts."

"But I thought that was good for your economy. The tourists pay the medicine men well."

"Phoenix Rising, the Navajo Nation is not a theme park. That is what the casinos are for."

There was a new voice. "Blue Wolf, this is Mama Bear. Let me tell you, that from six thousand miles away, I can sense that this man has a good heart…and to prolong the life of a man such as this would be a great benefit to the DiNé and to all the people of the world."

Blue Wolf dug in. "We have already bent tribal law for Phoenix Rising. We must not break it. Caring Arms, do you have anything to say on this matter?"

The young medicine man spoke up. "I would go to Rome, but only with the blessing of the council."

Blue Wolf stated, "If there are no more voices, then we will now vote. All delegates in favor of sending Caring Arms to Rome, raise a hand to your camera."

No hands were raised.

"All opposed?"

All hands were raised.

Blue Wolf concluded, "The matter is settled. Phoenix Rising, please send our deepest condolences to the pope and his followers. This meeting is adjourned."

We watched glumly as each square went blank on my laptop. Only two faces remained, those of Caring Arms and Blue Wolf.

Surprisingly, Blue Wolf spoke again. "Caring Arms, I am now ordering you to go to Rome to perform a healing ceremony on the pope. You are to leave as soon as possible. Take all necessary precautions to protect your identity. If you are successful, then Phoenix Rising, or Saint Carli as they call her, must take one hundred percent of the credit for healing the pope."

All of us were in total shock. "But why would you say this?" I asked. "Why would you break tribal law?"

"Dr. Bill knows why," replied Blue Wolf. "Now go."

Blue Wolf's square on the screen went blank. I asked, "Bill, can you tell us?"

"No," replied our cousin. "That would be a violation of HIPAA laws and I could lose my medical license."

"Well, I don't have a medical license," said Caring Arms. "Blue Wolf had colon cancer and didn't know it until we used a hundred thousand dollars of the pope's gift to purchase colonoscopy equipment...and Dr. Bill used it to save his life."

"But why didn't *you* try to save him?" I asked my 'brother.'"

"Because Blue Wolf wouldn't trust his life to a rookie medicine man. I've still never led a healing ceremony."

"Oh, great," I moaned.

I tried to point out, "Okay, the pope has only about five or six hours left and it would take fifteen hours to get there from Chinle. Caring Arms, my brother, I have to ask you an unpleasant question. Has a medicine man ever raised the dead?"

"No, and it would be a great taboo to even try. Stay away from witchcraft."

"Could you fly in the second seat of a military jet."

In the little square on the screen, Caring Arms shook his head. "There has to be at least four of us. Little Bear will play the drum while Mama Bear and Bluebird sing. Rising Sun never did it with less."

I mulled over our diminishing options and said, "Let me get back to you guys. I'm going to try to make some calls...bye."

"Calls to who?" Dad asked me.

"I'm Googling 'fastest jet in the world' and see what we can come up with."

I began clicking away. "The fastest fighter jet is the Mikoyan Gurevich 31 Foxhound at 1,900 mph, miles per hour."

Dad told me, "We're off to a bad start. An MG? That's a MiG. It's a Russian plane."

"Okay, how about the Lockheed SR-71 Blackbird reconnaissance plane… that one flies at up to 2,455 mph."

"Where is it located?"

"Uh, it's hanging from the ceiling at the Smithsonian. Let me try to get a better one…Okay, here's the McDonnell Douglas F-15 Eagle which flies at 1,875 mph, that's good. It's in service and would go Chinle to Rome in about three hours…range is three thousand miles."

Dad commented, "So it would have to refuel once, probably in the Azores…and we'd need five planes, one for you and four for the four Navajos…because these jets are just two-seaters, aren't they?"

"Let me see…uh, no, they just have one seat, Dad."

I smacked my forehead with my hand.

"Dad, what if we called one of the civilian aerospace companies? Their vehicles travel at least 17,000 mph."

"But wouldn't they need time to get ready…putting a rocket on the launch pad, fueling it up, manning the mission control, fitting us with space suits and training us…and even if they had one waiting for us now, where would we have to fly to?"

"They launch from Cape Canaveral and Texas," I replied.

"So add more flying time for that…and the passengers land by parachute, so what if the wind blows us far away from the pope's hospital? This whole thing is starting to remind me of the *Star Trek* episode that had the Kobayashi Maru…a no-win scenario."

"But Dad, Captain Kirk didn't believe in no-win scenarios."

"I see. So if you were Captain Kirk, what would you do?"

"Cheat of course…but that won't work here. Maybe we should look for a plane that doesn't exist."

"I don't follow you."

"Well, I saw this item on the news last week—"

"Wait a minute, you were watching the news?"

"At Grandma's house. They said there were private groups out there currently developing hypersonic aircraft."

"You mean supersonic."

"No, Dad…hypersonic aircraft go faster, a way lot faster. They said they could fly from L.A. to Tokyo in two hours…and the prototypes have already been developed. They're flying now, probably at night because no one has ever seen one. That's why they're called ghost planes."

"Carli, if you're right, then our military should know about them even if they're not the ones doing the building. But how would we go up the chain of command?"

Laura asked, "Don't you have the number of the FBI guy?"

I told Mom, "I have it, but that's really starting from the bottom. Still, by now everyone knows that the pope is dying, and saving his life should be a top priority. Okay, so Zimblist calls the head of the FBI, who calls the President, who calls the Chairman of the Joint Chiefs…and that's the guy who should know if there's a plane somewhere in the world that can be the pope's lifeboat."

* * *

The only thing worse than waiting is waiting and not knowing, as the pope's window of life drew down to four to five hours. My stress had manifested itself into many of the classic bodily symptoms…anxiety, muscle tension, headaches, dizziness, shaking, nausea, rapid heartbeat, high blood pressure, shortness of breath, low energy, pessimism, nail biting, fidgeting, pacing, ringing in my ear, ringing in my cell phone—

"CARLI! ANSWER YOUR PHONE!" screamed my mom.

I pressed the speaker button, and nervously said, "Hello."

The voice on the other end had a distinctive southern drawl. "Y'all call for a taxi?"

"A hypersonic taxi!" I yelled at the phone.

"Got *that* right," the man replied. "My name is Caesar Von Bettencourt. I'm the billionaire no one's ever heard of 'cause I don't stick my face in front of a camera every five minutes. I heard y'all need a fast ride to save the pope… and being an old Eagle Scout, I'm ready to do a good turn. My prototype does fly, but first we have to have an understanding. This is a 'ghost' plane. It doesn't exist. So if y'all are asked, you never saw it and you never heard of it. Are we clear on that?"

"Absolutely," I agreed. "So how fast can this non-existent plane travel?"

"We can get her up to Mach 4 if we 'prime the pump.'"

"How much is that in American numbers?" I asked.

"A smidge over three thousand miles per hour, with a range of seven thousand miles."

"Great!" I said, smiling and pumping my fist. "But how many of us can you take?"

"Payload is two pilots and a dozen passengers. Now before the pope slips away, why don't y'all give me the pickup?"

As fast as I could talk, I told him, "There're two stops. The first one is Chinle, Arizona, seven people, but the runway is pretty short."

"Well, as Doc Brown would say in *Back to the Future*, 'Where we're going, we don't *need* runways.' My own plane is a jump jet, like the Harrier...does vertical takeoffs and landings. Just find me a landing spot big enough for a helicopter."

"The football field at the high school!" I yelled again. "Do you need the address?"

"No, I've got great GPS. Tell your party I'll be there in fifteen minutes... and no luggage; we'll be back by nightfall. Where's the second stop?"

"Our house," I said, "but you'll need a place to land. The dog park is pretty close."

"And where's that?" asked Caesar.

"Shaker Boulevard at Richmond Road in Beachwood," I replied.

"Dumb question, dear, but what state?"

"OHIO!" all three of us yelled.

"Got it. Just make sure to shoo all them little doggies away before I get there, or they're gonna' get a hot foot...Now let's see, Chinle to Beachwood is 1,547 miles, at 3,069 miles per hour...that's exactly thirty minutes, plus the first stop. So I will see you folks in fifty minutes, that's five-oh minutes, with another 1.5 hours there to Rome, and don't be tardy."

"When are you leaving?" I asked.

"I've already got wheels off the ground out of Vandenberg Air Force Base, north of L.A. Let's get moving...Out."

I quickly dialed up our cousin. He answered on the first ring.

"Yes."

"Bill, this is not a joke. You have ten minutes to get all seven of you to the football field with the healing 'stuff,' to board a ghost plane...and no suitcases. We'll be back by night."

"What the heck is a ghost plane?"

"You'll meet a fellow pilot. And the first rule of ghost plane is 'You do not talk about ghost plane.' And Bill, Caring Arms should kindly remember to bring his pendant, the one with the black healing stone. You guys should probably use the bathroom first too. You have nine minutes."

"We're on our way, Carli."

I hung up and placed my next call. It too, was answered on the first ring.

"Romano."

"Is the pope still alive?"

"Yes, but not for long. He has lost consciousness."

"How long? I need an estimate."

I heard Monsignor Romano exhale deeply and he said, "Three hours, perhaps four at best."

"Are you at Gemelli Hospital, and do they have a helipad?"

"Yes to both."

"Okay, we'll be there in…" With the palm of my right hand, I smacked the side of my forehead several times. As a store manager, I was supposed to be good in math…1.5 plus .5 plus fifteen minutes…"Okay, meet us at the helipad in two hours and fifteen minutes. Bring ten jackets with pullover hoods…we need total secrecy. Once we arrive, all hospital personnel must leave the operating room."

"All shall be done as you say, Saint Carli…and thank you for your efforts. Andare con Dio."

126

EIGHTEEN

"Let's get our black wigs on. We need to leave now."

At 11:00 a.m., I stood in the middle of "Barkwood," Beachwood's dog park. It was a beautiful Sunday morning and maybe eighteen or twenty dogs raced past me. I raised my arms, and yelled as loud as I could.

"Can I have everyone's attention please? In a few minutes, a jump jet will be landing in the park. It's extremely dangerous and everyone needs to get their pet and leave now."

All present just laughed at me, including Godzilla's owner, Dale. He scoffed, "In that case, I think I'll stay and see the show."

"No, seriously, it's dangerous," I argued. But my powers of persuasion seemed lacking.

"Is he landing on the little side or the big side?" asked Dale.

"The big side."

"As long as his dog is over thirty pounds, I don't see a problem."

I walked away from him and scanned the skies...still nothing. Then I started hearing a jet engine...and its decibels increased rapidly. I suddenly realized he wasn't coming toward us, but instead, falling on top of us from above...and this object was dropping like a rock.

Panic ensued, but not a normal panic. The bond between dog and human is so strong, that it might even be classified as the fifth fundamental force in the universe. Most humans will willingly risk their own life to save the life of their dog.

Owners sprinted, and hollered out the names of their beloved pets against the roar of the machine above them. "Roni! Scout! Enzo! Gibbs! Crispy! Cooper! Lilly! Archie! Yana! Cleo! Otto-Shmotto! Gloria! Rico! Maggie! Annie! Juneau! Charlie! Strudel! Albus! Zoe! Luna! Rufus! Max! Godzilla!"

For a precious minute, Caesar let the ghost plane hover about a hundred feet off the ground, with engines pointed downward. He would not harm any canines even to save the pope. This gave me a brief moment to study the appearance of a plane that did not exist.

It certainly looked *stealthy*...a collection of straight lines except for the two engines. And I remembered seeing a similar plane, the F117 Nighthawk at the Cleveland Air Show a few years ago. But the needle-nosed fuselage of the ghost plane had no windows, and looked much more alien than the Nighthawk. I would not be surprised if it became the source of many UFO sightings during our flight to Rome.

Once cleared, Caesar let the craft fall the remaining distance to the ground. I was sure his seven passengers "lost their stomachs" in the freefall even though the landing was gentle.

We rushed to the plane as our cousin lowered a seven-foot metal ladder, not a very luxurious entryway for such a remarkable craft.

It was ladder down, ladder up in less than fifteen seconds. "Move it! Move it!" Bill ordered and he practically pushed us toward the back seats past Mama Bear and her whole clan. "Buckle up! Wheels up!" he yelled. Then he sprinted forward.

I blinked twice. Bill was riding shotgun with Caesar? But Bill's plane was powered by a rubber band compared to this vehicle.

"UUUUUUUUUHHHHHHHHHHuuuuuuuuhhhhhhhhhh!!!"

The G-forces kicked in so fast on takeoff, I was not prepared to feel the skin peeling back on my face. And the cabin was already getting warmer due to friction with the air. Our pilot was obviously in a hurry to get up to 3,000 mph…and I had to say that was a *good* thing.

After about ten minutes, I could feel the plane leveling off, and now there seemed to be no motion at all. With no windows, it felt like we were sitting in a small room. So I decided to be brave and get out of my seat.

"Are you guys okay?" I asked Mama Bear's clan of six.

"It's great!" said eight-year-old Little Bear. "It's just like a roller coaster."

I looked at Caring Arms. In a deadpan voice I asked him, "Can you perform the ceremony without Rising Sun?" But I was not at all comfortable with his response.

"Phoenix…………………………………………I don't know."

Next, I walked to the doorless cockpit and peered in at the multiple arrays of digital screens. "So you guys don't have any windows either?" I asked.

Our host tapped one of his touchscreens. "This camera shows us we're now passing over Manhattan."

My astonishment was evident. "But we've only been flying for ten minutes."

My cousin turned and smiled at me. "Carli, I've got to get me a ride like this…except the neighbors might get ticked off by the sonic booms."

I raised an eyebrow. "Can you actually fly this thing?"

"All planes operate by the same general aerodynamic principles. Maybe Caesar's got a few more bells and whistles, but it doesn't take me long to catch on."

"How high are we?" I inquired.

Caesar answered, "About a hundred thousand feet. That's about nineteen miles. Any higher and there'd be no oxygen for the engines. Any lower at this speed and we'd burn up in the atmosphere. That's why the plane's made of titanium. It can stand extreme temperatures. And its lighter weight allows us to fly a longer range at a higher altitude. Have you ever heard of titanium?"

"Yes, I believe they use it in spinal surgeries...Do you have any other heat shields?"

"The best—Buckypaper, an aggregate of carbon nanotubes."

"You lost me."

"Well, look at it this way...It's fifty thousand times thinner than a human hair and five hundred times stronger than steel...a lot better than those tiles used on the Space Shuttle. That's why we were able to accelerate so much on the way up."

I told Caesar, "Yeah, I really felt those G-forces."

"Ha! Those were baby G's...maybe two or three. The Millennium Force at Cedar Point pulls 4.5 G's. You probably wouldn't ride it."

"You're right...So are we in space?"

"Space doesn't start till mile marker sixty-two, but here, on this screen you can at least see the curvature of the earth. I've got no windows, but cameras and radar are everywhere."

"But what about—"

"You know, Dr. Bill, your cousin Carli asks a lot of questions."

Bill nodded. "Next, she'll want to see your parachutes."

"Oh, they're in the rear storage."

My cousin and I both looked at Caesar with wide eyes.

The pilot spread his hands. "What? I'm serious. I keep fourteen parachutes in rear storage...enough for everyone. This is an experimental airplane."

"How long have you been flying it?" I asked.

"Well, in three weeks, it'll be...two months."

* * *

"STRAP IN, EVERYONE!" called the pilot. "WE'RE COMING IN HOT! TOUCHDOWN IN TEN MINUTES!"

Caesar was right. Atmospheric friction was starting to make the cabin feel like a sweat lodge. The reason there were no windows, I figured, was because he didn't want the passengers seeing the plane's heat shield burning up.

"LANDING GEAR DEPLOYED! NOW DOING A STRAIGHT DROP FROM FIFTEEN THOUSAND FEET! HOLD ON!"

I didn't sign up for skydiving. I knew I had done something like this once before. What was the name of that ride?…Oh, yeah…Tower of Terror at Disney World. Great ride, but my faulty brain kept telling me I was going to get crushed when we hit bottom. I received no award for surviving.

"Mama! Look at us! We're flying!"

Little Bear and Little Lamb laughed so hard and couldn't get enough of the fun. They floated a few inches above their seats and watched their arms levitate. Even I had to admit they looked cute pretending to be airplanes flying in our weightless environment even though they were strapped in.

When Caring Arms realized he was missing something important, he reached up and snatched his pendant out of the air…and a few seconds later, our weightless joyride ended.

"UUUUHHHHuuuuhhhh!" With a thud, my blood starting flowing back to the proper places.

The pilot shouted, "WHEELS DOWN! EVERYONE OUT! MOVE IT! MOVE IT!"

My cousin sprang from his seat and lowered the metal ladder. "Help upstairs," he asked me. Then he went down first and made sure all de-planed safely. Caesar remained aboard, and everyone stretched. It was 6:00 p.m. in Rome and still light outside.

I looked around and saw a great sight…a platoon of the pope's men rushing toward us with hooded spring jackets. It was extremely important to keep the Navajo's identities a secret.

Monsignor Romano ran up and grabbed my arm. "The pope is alive," he said breathlessly, "maybe for an hour…All hospital personnel are being escorted out of his operating room as we speak."

In Arizona, I would defer to the judgment of Mama Bear and Bill. But in Rome, because of my relationship with the Vatican, I had to take charge of our small party.

"Hoods up and move fast!" I called out.

In the Olympic sport of race-walking, all of us were now competitors. I don't want to say that Monsignor Romano lacked dignity, huffing and puffing ahead of us, but his disheveled attire made a great visual target for us to follow…and down the corridors he led us.

The pope's emissary made a quick right turn and bashed through a swinging door with his shoulder. Behind him, I stopped dead in my tracks at the operating table. The doctors had left the pope "as is."

"Mama Bear," I snapped, "have the two little kids sit on the floor. They shouldn't see this."

What I saw, I couldn't comprehend. I had to remind myself that this was a human being...and he was still alive, but I wasn't sure how. Everything in his abdominal cavity was a bloody mess. I couldn't identify a single organ. A breathing tube was lodged in his throat. Even Bill's face turned ashen white. We knew that my injuries were child's play compared to this...and we brought a medicine man with zero experience at healing.

I turned to my host. "Monsignor Romano, I must please ask you to leave now. Andare con Dio."

He replied, "Andare con Dio," and left the room.

"Okay, folks," I called out. "Let's lose the jackets and take our places."

I asked Bill, "Don't we have to remove all the tubes and clamps from the pope's body?"

"Carli, your spinal hardware vanished, so let's not touch a thing."

Caring Arms brought a compass and stationed himself south of the pope. Mama Bear and her daughters took up southwest positions, with Little Lamb sitting with the gourd rattle. Little Bear sat north with his tom-tom and the prayer sticks were placed east. The rest of us, including Red Bear, moved to the far back corner.

Dad caught Mom off guard by planting a wet one on her lips, a deep kiss lasting several seconds. "This time you'll get to see it," he told her.

"We hope," she replied.

I pointed my finger at Mama Bear and said, "Showtime."

Then we waited...and waited...and I was starting to get really nervous because nothing was happening. Mama Bear and Bluebird were singing the "Night Chant," the two kids were playing their instruments, and Caring Arms was...well, yes he was holding the black stone with both hands, and he closed his eyes, but I couldn't understand why he was wrenching his jaw.

I dared not speak to him. He was oddly twisting his mouth as if he was trying to force a yawn.

Dad whispered, "I never saw Rising Sun doing that."

Warning tones suddenly came alive around the pope's body. I was sure these were not good signs. The worst was the alarm sounded by the sustained high pitch of the electrocardiogram. The steady blips had stopped. What was left of the pope's heart was flatlining.

In desperation, I whispered to our cousin, "Can you shock him back with the defibrillator? You're a doctor. Can't you do something?"

131

Bill smacked the back of his hand against me. "Don't do a thing," he whispered back angrily.

Then this had to be the end. Caring Arms said himself he would not try to heal a dead man. Still, his concentration was evident...and Mama Bear hadn't stopped singing. The drum, the rattle...everyone sustained the "Event." Then a few seconds later, something did happen.

"Whoa! There it is! There it is!" came my loudest whisper ever. The feeling was magical. It was much brighter than I had ever imagined it would be. Millions of bright streaks formed a solid wall of light in the shape of a human that descended from near the ceiling.

The EKG resumed its rhythmic blipping of the pope's beating heart as the lasers deftly created a superhighway for the coming mist.

This was the show we had been hoping for. Four members in the Navajo healing party broke out into wide smiles, while our new medicine man settled into a relaxed concentration and calm breathing.

After a few minutes, the light dimmed and the mist took over right on schedule. This was the part that I least understood. Our cousin explained to me once that individual water molecules could only exist as steam, and it would take 1.5 sextillion of them to fit in a drop of water. As I watched, I wished that I could reach out and touch un-wet water.

"Did you see that, Carli?" said Bill. "The two bullets just popped out and landed on the floor."

"I thought they were supposed to dissolve like the titanium."

"Not if they're loose and not attached to anything. Look again. There goes the breathing tube, a set of clamps, now the IV drip...Anything not human is gone. So are you ready for the main event?"

I was in awe. "Bill, this is so amazing, and to think that you and we three are the only Caucasians to ever see it."

"Let's make sure it stays that way. Look up, Carli. Here comes stage three."

Now I could see the real beauty in what Bill had earlier told me that he liked to call a "box of atoms" as it made its way down from the ceiling...and again, assumed the shape of the patient. I agreed that these bright sparklers looked like a *Star Trek* transporter in action, but they weren't stationary like the light and the mist. What I observed was a movement playing in reverse, similar to when a kid does a cannonball dive off the high-board and creates a big splash. If you play that movie backward, everything comes back in graceful arcs to the point of impact...in this case, the point of impact being the man on the operating table.

132

We were all mesmerized watching the miracle unfold before us. One by one, human organs became recognizable again…the heart, the lungs, the liver…then the ribcage was reassembled…and finally, the outer skin was molded shut without a hint of a scar.

In the next split second, everything in the room just stopped at once—the sparklers, the singing, and the instruments.

In exhaustion, Caring Arms dropped to one knee, and Mama Bear rushed to his aid. We five spectators back in the corner looked at each other for a moment, and then we looked at the pope. Since he was visibly breathing on his own, we decided to slowly walk toward the operating table. Then came a shock.

"AHHHHHHH!" I'm not sure who in our party screamed. Maybe it was all of us, but it was totally unnecessary. The pope just did a sit-up…and not a gentle sit-up. This was the robust kind you would do when you're competing in gym class.

He apparently didn't remember where he was. With an inquisitive expression, the pontiff blinked his eyes several times and then looked around at the room and his ten companions.

He took a deep breath, getting ready to speak. "You know, I've often had dreams like this," he said, "where I wake up in public wearing only my underwear."

I ran to get him a hospital gown, while Dad ran to let Monsignor Romano into the room.

When I returned, the pope grabbed my right wrist. "Saint Carli," he said, "God told me you would not let me down."

"I had a lot of help, Your Holiness."

The pope looked at Caring Arms and winked an eye. The now experienced medicine man came forward to reply and he was greeted by a raucous round of applause. I called out, "Not bad for a rookie!"

Caring Arms spoke softly. "Mr. Pope, sir, the Navajo Nation respectfully requests that all credit for this Event goes to Phoenix Rising…or Saint Carli as you call her."

The pope nodded. "Well, since I was not awake during the Event, then I suppose I'll have to take your word for it…that is, provided Saint Carli concurs with your assessment."

I donned a pair of latex gloves so I could legally hug my ceremonial brother…then doffed them for Mama Bear, Little Bear, Little Lamb, Bluebird, and Red Bear. "I accept full responsibility for the Event, Your Holiness."

The pope smiled. "We have a *vinco-vinci*, or as you Americans say, a win-win. Good for the Navajo Nation and good for the Church."

I took Caring Arms aside and asked him, "Why were you contorting your jaw at the beginning?"

"Rising Sun trained me that putting pressure on the inner ear helps focus mind and spirit. So I tried to squeeze my eustachian tubes the same way we do it on an elevator or airplane. The problem is, trying to hold it for ten minutes is brutal. No wonder he needed time to recover."

"I was afraid it was over when the pope's heart stopped beating. You said yourself that you wouldn't try to heal a dead man."

"He wasn't dead. His spirit hadn't yet left his body."

"But how did you know that?"

"Come on, Carli, we're Navajos. The women kept singing and the kids kept playing. We *all* knew it."

"So then how was Rising Sun able to walk away from my ceremony after he had transferred his spirit to me?"

The young man scanned our surroundings and led me to a laptop on a high stand. Then he punched up a video, ironically, the same one that Mandy had showed me; everyone walking down the ICU hallway.

"Carli, if you look closely, you can see my right hand under Rising Sun's left armpit, and Dr. Bill's left hand under the right armpit. He didn't weigh very much, maybe a hundred pounds, so it looked like he was walking out with us."

"Are you saying that before you left the ICU, Rising Sun was already—"

"Yes, Carli, he had already entered the fourth world…and that is why Dr. Bill said we had to leave quickly."

"WE HAVE TO LEAVE QUICKLY, PEOPLE!" Bill yelled to all. "I got a call from Caesar…The meter's running on our ghost plane."

"Wait!" the pope interrupted. "Saint Carli, come over to me."

I complied.

He reached out for my hand again. "I have not yet finished Sunday mass. I would be greatly honored if you would return with me and stand in the window at my side."

I looked in my parents' direction. There was no debate. "Of course, kiddo," Dad answered.

Then I turned to my cousin. "Bill, can you escort Mama Bear and family back to Chinle? It should only take two hours. We'll find our own way home."

"Absolutely. Hey, great job digging up that ghost plane today, Carli. To think you guys were once nervous about flying in my puddle-jumper."

"Also," I added, "please extend a thousand thank-yous to Caesar Von Bettencourt. He's still an unknown billionaire, but today, as an Eagle Scout, he did his good turn."

"HáGOóNEé, Farewell," we said to our favorite Navajo family…and they echoed those words to us as they departed.

"Romano!" the pope called. "You will bring your personal car to the nearest exit and drive us back to the Vatican. Tell no one."

"But Your Holiness, you are wearing only a hospital gown."

"So? If they see my *culo*, that's the way God made me…Do as I ask now." The emissary bowed. "As you wish."

* * *

It was dark when we re-entered the Vatican through the northern back entrance at 8:00 p.m. We piled out of the car and into two golf carts that took us around the Basilica and back to the Sacristy. There, I was handed the same white robe that I wore last time.

The pope and I wasted no time in the changing rooms and both of us re-appeared five minutes later just as we had looked on the day of my ceremony.

Stunned Vatican employees stared wide-eyed at the two of us as we marched quickly through the Basilica while transistor radios blared out the breaking news.

"OSPEDALE DICE MANCA IL CORPO DEL PAPA!" (HOSPITAL REPORTS THE BODY OF THE POPE IS MISSING!)

It was not missing for long.

Monsignor Romano led us to the top floor of the Apostolic Palace and down the corridor to a room where the pope's balcony window was still open and still proudly hanging a bloodstained papal flag in front.

As millions below us were holding a candlelight vigil to mourn the pope, he and I stepped forward together.

At first, maybe the crowd thought he was an apparition. Then index fingers began pointing upward at the window, followed by the cries of "PAPA! PAPA!"

And then came my favorite vocabulary word, *catharsis:* (noun) An explosive release of emotional tension, after an overwhelming experience, that restores and refreshes the spirit.

The joyous sounds of every church bell pealed out in Rome, while fifteen miles to the southeast, the National Institute of Geophysics and Volcanology reported a moderate earthquake registering 4.0 on the Richter scale...caused by three million people dancing in the streets.

NINETEEN

I asked to stay five additional days to do more "ministering" in the Sistine Chapel, and Mom reminded me, "Don't forget to have Cassie call in sick at work."

All went well, though I did have a bit of pickle trying to explain to the pope why his wisdom teeth came back.

And as we packed our bags to leave Rome, the sniper who shot the pope was captured by Interpol using facial recognition software when he tried to flee the country. They determined he was a lone wolf anarchist and not part of a larger organization.

"What's this?" I asked, bending down to retrieve an envelope delivered under the door of our guest suite. I read it aloud.

"To the Green family: His Holiness kindly requests the honor of your presence for dinner in Audience Hall this evening at 6:00. Monsignor Romano will escort you."

"Dress-up time again," Dad said, reopening his bag for the wrinkled suit he had purchased on Monday. "Caesar said no luggage, and like sheep, we had listened to him."

At 5:50, our favorite emissary picked us up with the comment, "You have created much confusion at Gemelli Hospital. Every baby girl born there this week has been named Carli." He then led us to Audience Hall, which was actually just next door to Saint Martha's Guest House. The place looked big, and he told us it could seat over six thousand people, but tonight's dinner would be a little more intimate.

"Saint Carli," he said, "I want you to take a peek in the door before we enter the Hall...and tell me what you see."

Monsignor Romano held the door ajar as I took in the scene. I responded, "I see the pope on the stage and I see several hundred people eating dinner on the main floor."

"Saint Carli," he said quietly, "this is the reason we take our miracles so seriously, but these people are *your* miracles. Every one of those persons is either a patient or the relative of a patient whom you blessed during your five-week sabbatical in the Sistine Chapel. Of the 23,040 persons you met, 235 of them reported spontaneous remission of their disease after you touched them. So, including the healing of the pope, you are now credited with performing 239 miracles...and they are all here tonight because they want to thank you."

I buried my face against my mom's chest and sobbed, "But I didn't do anything."

"You did much, Saint Carli. So many illnesses are psychosomatic in nature. That means that things such as stress, fear, worry, anxiety, loneliness, and depression can all cause physical symptoms leading to chronic illness."

"You couldn't see it at the time, but many of these people were suffering from high blood pressure, respiratory problems, gastro-intestinal issues, migraine headaches, infertility, and every form of cancer, which by the way has only a one in one hundred thousand chance of going into remission on its own. But for those you touched, it was one in one hundred."

Monsignor Romano snapped his fingers. "Saint Carli, there is someone I would like you to meet."

An eight-year-old boy and his parents were brought through the door. The little boy immediately hugged me.

The emissary pointed out, "You might not recognize him. When you switched over to the 'Saint Carli rules,' he was your first visitor. You weren't even sure if he was a boy or girl...but he had leukemia and now it is gone."

The parents offered heartfelt thanks of "Grazie, grazie."

Monsignor Romano stated firmly, "By touching these people in need, you gave them the will to live; the will to fight back...You gave them the Carli mojo."

* * *

We slept well. It was now time to return home (on a sub-Mach Vatican chartered flight) and resume our mundane, but satisfying lives as the Johnson family. We thought it a good idea to hire an agent to handle the Patron Saint of Buckeyes merchandise sales. My alter ego, Saint Carli, was making so many millions that I could hardly give it all away fast enough...with a good portion of the donations going to burn patient groups, especially those for children.

One thing, however, did change in a big way...and that was the public's perception when they saw me standing in the window with a very much alive pope. All interviews, lectures, and TV shows still portraying Carli Green as a hoaxer were cancelled—permanently.

So Dr. Dred and Dr. Duncan lived unhappily ever after...and that was fine with me.

EPILOGUE

I waited over a decade to write this story because the first part is true. My daughter did lose her husband in the fire and received the injuries described. The x-ray photo is her actual spinal x-ray. At the time of publication, she is doing fairly well and gave me permission to write the story. We both graduated from The Ohio State University and she did work in a sandwich shop across the street from the hospital. The two crazy doctors are completely fictional. My family received exceptional care from every staff member at The Ohio State University Wexner Medical Center. (And yes, the hospital does have a prison ward on the eighth floor.) The character of Dr. Bill Green is mostly true. My cousin did work as a physician on the Navajo Reservation in Tuba City and flew his own airplane. The characters Roland, Laura, and Carli Green are partially true representations of my family. All other characters in the story are fictional and all names used in the story are fictional.

Being a Clevelander with a baseball team name change, I am very aware of the importance of showing respect for Native Americans. I researched many sources through websites, books, and phone calls to insure that what I wrote was as accurate as possible. Wally Brown's YouTube videos were excellent. The Navajo Nation Museum was also very helpful, as was the website "Tony Hillerman Portal," and the personal experiences of my cousin who lived on the Reservation. To the best of my knowledge, the Navajo words used in the book are accurate. The photo of the Navajo family, in addition to most other photos are licensed through iStock.com. Being fiction, parts of the story will not be authentic, mainly the three ceremonies … healing, adoption, and anointing. They were also abbreviated to keep the story moving along. The Night Chant is real, but abbreviated and in a different order.

The pope does not represent any particular pope. The Vatican buildings noted are real and most of my information came from Mother Teresa's canonization seen on YouTube, along with websites concerning qualifications for sainthood.

My Mother's Daughter

(This is the actual letter written by my daughter to my wife a few months after the fire. Only the names have been changed.)

Mom,

I remember when I was a little girl, you wrote a poem to your mom thanking her for being your mom and raising you. Now it is my turn to do the same. You gave me life and saved my life. There's nothing I could do to thank you enough. I'm so lucky to have you, the best mom in the whole world.

I had the best childhood any kid could ask for. You did your best to protect me from the world. I love the home movies that my brother has been posting to the Internet. It brings me back to an innocent and joyous time.

As I grew into my teens, I longed for independence. I felt I needed to experience things for myself, good or bad, right or wrong. I know this transition proved to be difficult for both of us.

When Marty came into my life, you became more open and accepting of him which in turn, helped our relationship rebuild. I felt like Marty became our bridge that took both of us back to those innocent days of my childhood. Now, after this terrible tragedy, you have not judged me or made me feel ashamed, but rather opened your heart to me and took me back under your wing. I could not have survived without you.

And now in return, I promise to become a better person and daughter to you. I will shed this cocoon skin and flourish into a beautiful butterfly.

I want you to take care of me and in return, one day, I will take care of you. I am so excited to share with you all of the things we have learned while apart from each other, and to share this new open and supportive relationship with you.

I am proud to say I am my mother's daughter.

Love always,

Carli

Rick Fishman's debut novel, *Sandlot Summit*, is a rip-roaring baseball comedy ideal for ages 9 to 14.

It's 1984, and the cold war between the United States and the Soviet Union is heating up to a fever pitch. With combat a near certainty, President Ronald Reagan and the infamous Russian General, Kostlitzo "Boneface" Zolotov, make a secret pact to settle differences, not by fighting a war, but instead, by playing a kids' baseball game. Twelve-year-old center fielder, Fredder Farley, is chosen to head the American squad and every step in the journey will test his mettle as a leader. With his dad as coach, he and his friends must find a way to save the free world from conquest by what President Reagan calls— the "Evil Empire."

About the Author

Rick Fishman's last trip to Rome was a disaster. He was coerced into fighting a gladiator duel against the infamous barbarian Hideus Maximus … and performed so poorly that even his wife, Lynn, turned against him and voted thumbs down, rooting for her husband's demise.

Rick is an Ohio State Buckeye alum and had a split career as an accountant and math teacher, and is currently retired … enjoying family time at home reading, writing, walking the dog, and feeding the squirrels. He and his wife have two adult children. *The Navajo Event* is Rick's second novel, following his kids' baseball comedy *Sandlot Summit*.

Living in Cleveland, Rick coached youth baseball in Lyndhurst, Ohio for 12 years and has been a volunteer in the Big Brothers/Big Sisters Association since 2013. In 1992, Rick earned a spot in the Guinness Book of Records by painting the world's largest map at Rowland Elementary School in South Euclid, Ohio.

Facebook page: Facebook.com/Rick.Fishman.9

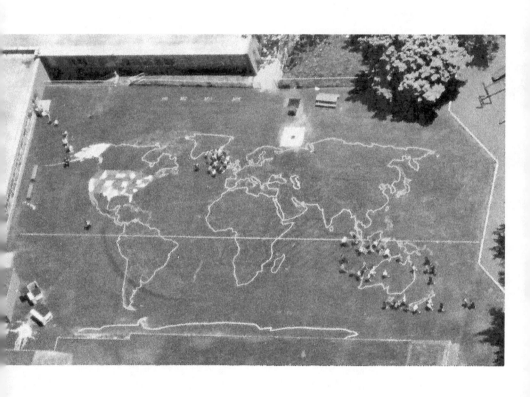

CPSIA information can be obtained
at www.ICGtesting.com
Printed in the USA
BVHW041435020522
635886BV00023B/534